"You asked me to come if I changed my mind."

Deborah rushed on nervously, "Well I have. But if you don't want to marry me now, I'll understand...."

"I still want to marry you." Gideon smiled a little. "My daughter will be delighted, and for that matter, so am I." His mouth twisted in a wry smile. "I should have said that sooner, shouldn't I?"

"Why should you? We mustn't pretend, must we?" Deborah blushed brightly because, of course, her whole life was going to be one long pretence from that moment.

"Most sensibly spoken. There's no reason to wait. I don't suppose you want to glide down the aisle in white satin, do you?" His eyes studied her face, and the blush, which was beginning to die down, took fresh fire.

She lied in a firm voice, "Oh no, nothing like that...."

Books by Betty Neels

HARLEQUIN ROMANCE

These books may be available at your local bookseller.

Don't miss any of our special offers. Write to us at the following address for information on our newest releases.

Harlequin Reader Service
P.O. Box 52040, Phoenix, AZ 85072-2040
Canadian address: P.O. Box 2800, Postal Station A,
5170 Yonge St., Willowdale, Ont. M2N 6J3

Year's Happy Ending

Betty Neels

Harlequin Books

TORONTO • NEW YORK • LONDON
AMSTERDAM • PARIS • SYDNEY • HAMBURG
STOCKHOLM • ATHENS • TOKYO • MILAN

Original hardcover edition published in 1984
by Mills & Boon Limited

ISBN 0-373-02692-7

Harlequin Romance first edition May 1985

CHAPTER ONE

THE September sun shone hazily on to the narrow garden. Its only occupant, who was busily weeding between the neat rows of vegetables, sat back on her knees and pushed her hair back from her forehead. Long hair, fine and straight and of a shade which could only be described as sandy. To go with the hair she had freckles, green eyes and long curling sandy lashes, startling in an otherwise ordinary face. She bent to her work once more, to be interrupted by her mother's voice from the open kitchen door: 'Your cousin Rachel wants you on the phone, Debby—she says it's important.'

Mrs Farley withdrew her head and Deborah dropped her trowel and ran up the garden, kicked off her sandals at the door and went into the hall. She picked up the receiver warily; Rachel was a dear and they were the best of friends, but she was frowned upon by the older members of the family, they didn't approve of her life. That she had held down a splendid job with some high powered executive was one thing, but her private goings on were something quite different. 'Hullo?' Deborah said, still wary, and her mother poked her head round the sitting room door to hiss:

'She can't come and stay—I have your Aunt Maud coming . . .'

But Rachel didn't want to come and stay, she spoke without preamble: 'Debby, you haven't got another job yet, have you? You're free . . .?'

'Yes, why?'

'You've heard me talk of Peggy Burns—you know, the girl who married some wealthy type with a house somewhere in Dorset? Well her mother's ill and she wants to go to her, only Bill—her husband—is in the Middle East or some such place and can't get back for a few weeks, and there are these kids—terrible twins, four years old, and the baby—just beginning to crawl. She's desperate for a nanny and I thought of you. Marvellous lolly, darling, and a gorgeous house. There's a housekeeper; rather elderly with bunions or housemaid's knee or something, and daily help from the village.'

'Where exactly does she live?' asked Deborah.

'Not far from you—Ashmore? Somewhere between Blandford and Shaftesbury. Do say you'll help out, Debby. Have you got your name down at an agency or something?'

'Well, yes—but I did say I intended to have a holiday before the next job.'

'Oh, good, so you can give them a ring and explain.' Rachel decided.

How like Rachel to skate over the bits she doesn't want to know about, thought Deborah; the phoning and explaining, the packing, the getting there . . . 'I haven't said I'll go,' she said a bit sharply.

Rachel's self-assured voice was very clear. 'Of course you'll go, Debby! Supposing it was your mother and no one would help you?'

'Why can't you go?' asked Deborah.

'I'm not a trained nanny, silly. Uncle Tom could run you over when he gets back from work; it's Coombe House, Ashmore, and here's the phone number so that you can ring and say you're coming.' Before Deborah could get her mouth open she went on

'I'm so grateful, darling, and so will Peggy be—bless you. I must fly—I've a new boy friend and he's taking me out this evening and I must wash my hair.'

'Rachel . . .' began Deborah, too late, her cousin had hung up.

Her mother said indignantly: 'But you've only been home a week darling, and the boys will be back for half term and you'll miss them. How like Rachel, arranging everything to suit herself without a thought . . .'

'Actually, she was trying to help,' said Deborah fairly, 'And I suppose I could go if its only for a week or two. I could ask the agency for a temporary job when I leave Ashmore and then be home for Christmas. I'd like that.'

Her mother brightened. 'That's true, love, and you haven't had a Christmas at home for a couple of years, have you? I don't know what your father will say . . .'

Deborah said gently, 'Mother, I'm twenty-three.'

'Yes, Debby I know, but your father always thinks of you as a little girl even though you're the eldest. He always will until you get married.'

'Mother,' said Deborah with faint exasperation. She would like to get married and have a husband and children and a home to run, but she considered her chances slight. She had plenty of friends for she had lived in Dorchester all her life, but most of them were married or thinking about it, and those who weren't, girl and man alike, tended to regard her as a well-liked sister to whom they could confide their amatory problems.

She sighed and went back to the phone.

The voice at the other end was pleasant, tinged with panic, but hopeful. 'Thank God,' said the voice fervently, 'Rachel said you'd ring, you've no idea . . .

you're like a miracle, I'd absolutely no idea what to do. I'm not usually such a fool, but I seem to have gone to pieces . . .'

Deborah heard a watery sigh and said hastily, 'I'll come just as soon as I can, Mrs Burns—my father will drive me over as soon as he gets home, that'll be in about two hours. Can you go to your mother this evening?'

'Yes, oh yes. She lives in Bath so I can drive myself. I'll get all ready to leave shall I? And put the twins to bed and see to the baby. You're an angel. I don't know your name, at least I'm sure Rachel told me but I don't think I took it in.'

'Deborah Farley. Is your house easy to find Mrs Burns?'

'Yes, oh yes. Facing the village green. There is a green gate that runs up to the side of the house, if you drive in and turn off to the front door.'

'About half-past seven, Mrs Burns. Goodbye until then.'

Deborah hung up. She would have to pack; uniform and white aprons and sensible shoes. She decided to take some summer clothes with her as well, off duty seemed a little unlikely but she could change in the evenings when the children were in bed. She went and told her mother and then made tea for them both, glancing with regret at the half weeded border she wouldn't have the time to finish now.

'I daresay it won't be for long,' she observed philosophically, 'I mean, Mrs Burns' mother will either get better or die, I hope she gets better, Mrs Burns sounds nice.'

'I wonder what the children will be like?' Her mother wanted to know doubtfully.

'No worse than some I've had to deal with,'

Deborah said cheerfully, 'and probably a good deal better. I'd better go and throw a few things into a bag.'

Her father wasn't best pleased, he had been looking forward to a quiet evening, reading the papers and watching the T.V. He was a kind-hearted man inclined to be taciturn at his work, managing one of the banks in Dorchester, and good at his job, but at the end of the day he was glad enough to get home, potter in the garden if he felt like it, and enjoy the peace and quiet of the evening. He looked at his daughter with faint annoyance.

'Really, Debby you are supposed to be on holiday.'

'Father dear I know, but this Mrs Burns is desperate and as I explained to mother, I could take a temporary job after I leave there and then come home for Christmas.' She kissed his cheek and smiled at him.

So he got out the car again and she said goodbye to her mother and Thomas the cat and got in beside him. 'It's quickest if you go to Blandford,' she suggested. 'It's on the Shaftesbury road then you can turn off to the right—I looked it up.'

The village, when they reached it, was charming, with its duckpond and the nice old houses clustered around it. And the house was easy enough to find, across the green with the wide gate standing invitingly open.

Mr Farley parked the car precisely before the door and they both got out. The house was stone built, square and Georgian, sheltered by old trees, its sash windows open. Deborah, her father beside her with her case, thumped the big brass knocker, not too loudly in case the children were asleep, and the door was flung open.

The young woman who stood there wasn't much older than herself, a good deal taller and very slim, with a short mop of fair curly hair and a pretty face. 'Oh, golly,' she breathed, 'I could hug you—you are an angel. Come in . . .' She looked at Mr Farley and Deborah said: 'This is my father, he drove me here.'

Mrs Burns smiled widely at him. She said earnestly: 'Nanny will be quite happy here, I do assure you Mr Farley, there's the housekeeper—she's getting supper actually, and there is plenty of daily help—it's just the children to look after. Come and have a drink . . .?'

Mr Farley, quite won over, said that no, he wouldn't as he had to drive back to Dorchester and his supper was to be waiting for him. He said goodbye to them both and got back into his car and drove off.

'He's nice,' observed Mrs Burns. 'My father died last year, he was nice too.' She wrinkled up her nose engagingly. 'You know—a bit fussy but always there. Of course, I've got Bill now, only he's not at home. He'll be back in a week or two though.'

She led the way across the hall into a comfortable room and waved Deborah to an easy chair. 'Do you mind if I don't stay for supper? I'll tell you as much as I can, then I'll be off . . . I'll leave my phone number so that you can ring every day. Mary—that's our housekeeper, will see to the house and the food and so on, she is a dear soul, but getting on a bit so the twins are a bit much for her. If you could cope with them and the baby she'll see to everything else.' She handed Deborah a glass of sherry and sat down herself. 'I'll tell you the routine . . .' She paused: 'Do you drive?'

'Oh, yes. Only I haven't a car.'

'Good. We all take it in turns to take the children to school. It's about a mile out of the village, mornings only; it won't be your turn until next week, anyway.'

'The baby's feeds?' prompted Deborah.

'Ah, yes.' Mrs Burns then dealt with them. 'And the baby's name is Deirdre, but we all call her Dee. The twins are Suzanne and Simon.' She added, with devastating honesty, 'They're awful, but not all the time.'

'How long do you expect to be away?' asked Deborah.

'I haven't an idea. 'A week, two . . . it depends.' She looked so sad for a moment that Deborah said quickly: 'Well, a week here or there doesn't matter much. I'm between jobs.'

Mrs Burns cast her a grateful glance. 'I'll never be able to thank you enough. Now here's the twins' routine . . .'

Within half an hour Deborah had been told all she wanted to know, been introduced to Mary, toured the house, peeped in on the twins and the baby in the nursery and shown her room next to it. A very nice room it was too; pastel pinks and blues and a thick carpet with the sort of bathroom Deborah had so often admired in glossy magazines. But she didn't waste time examining it instead she went back downstairs to where Mrs Burns was talking to Mary. She smiled as Deborah joined them.

'I'm going now, Mary's got your supper ready. There's one thing I forgot, she's going to a wedding in two days' time and she'll be away all day. Mrs Twist will be up from the village in the morning—could you cope for the rest of the day?'

Mrs Burns was looking anxious again so Deborah said bracingly: 'Of course I can, Mrs Burns, everything will be fine. I hope you find your mother better.' She urged her companion gently to the door and into the Porsche parked in the drive. A lovely car but surely not quite the right thing for a mother with three young children. Her thought was answered as though she had uttered it aloud. 'This isn't mine—it's Bill's second car. I've got a small Daimler, it's safer for the children he says. But I'm in a hurry now and they're not with me!'

'Go carefully,' urged Deborah.

Mrs Burns nodded obediently and shot off with the speed of light. Deborah watched her skid round into the road and went indoors, hoping that her employer was a seasoned driver. She ate her supper presently in the panelled dining room at the back of the house and then helped Mary clear away the dishes and wash up, and by then it was time to give Deirdre her ten o'clock feed. She sat in the day nursery with the baby on her lap; she took her feed like an angel and dropped off to sleep again as Deborah was changing her. It would be too much to expect the twins to be as placid, thought Deborah, climbing into her comfortable bed.

It was. She went along, next morning dressed in her uniform and a nicely starched apron, to see if they were awake and found the pair of them out of their beds and on the night nursery floor, busy covering the hearth rug with a wild pattern, wielding their felt pens with enthusiasm. She knelt down beside them, wished them good-morning and admired their handiwork. They both peered at her, two small artful faces with the same bright blue eyes as their little sister.

'You're the new Nanny,' said Simon without enthusiasm.

'Yes, I am, and you're Simon,' she smiled at the little girl, 'and you're Suzanne.'

'Is Mummy coming back soon?' asked the moppet.

'Just as soon as your granny is better. Mummy's going to phone today so you'll be able to speak to her.'

'Where's Daddy?'

Deborah wasn't sure if she'd been told—was it China or Japan? Anyway it was some far flung spot which would take a day or two to get home from, even if he started that very minute. 'I don't know exactly, you could ask Mummy, but I'm sure he'll be home just as soon as he can. Will you start to dress while I change Deirdre?'

'No.'

'Then if you're going to stay in your nightclothes, you'd better go to bed, hadn't you?' said Deborah calmly, and went over to see if the baby was awake.

'Will you tell Mummy if we're naughty?' asked Simon.

'I don't tell tales,' Deborah told him cheerfully, 'that's a nasty thing to do.'

'We'll get dressed,' said Suzanne, 'but I can't do my hair but I can tie a bow knot in my laces.'

'Clever girl. I'll do your hair when I've seen to Deirdre.'

Breakfast, though noisy, was eaten in a friendly atmosphere, and as soon as it was finished the twins were collected by someone they called Aunty Doris and driven off to school, leaving Deborah to bath and dress Dee, put her in her pram and wheel it round to the back of the house into a sheltered corner while she nipped back indoors to make beds and tidy the nurseries.

Mary, watching her put a load of small garments into the washing machine, approved of her. 'Plain she may be,' she confided to Mrs Twist, 'but she's a lady, if you know what I mean, and the twins mind her as

much as they mind anyone. Sitting there, telling them
in that soft voice of hers to eat their breakfast and so
sure she was they did too, like lambs! Pity we can't
have her here permanent like.'

The twins returned with a great deal of untapped
energy; Deborah combing hair and inspecting hands,
decided that a walk was essential after their dinner.
She left the twins playing while she saw to the baby
and then, with the infant tucked up in the pram and
the children armed with small baskets in case they
found any blackberries, set out.

They went through the village, stopping at the
stores to buy sweets and then took a lane beyond the
last of the houses. It led uphill and gave them a view
of rolling countryside when they reached the top.
Deborah, hot from pushing the pram, sighed with
relief to find a splendid hedge of blackberries, an
excuse to find a shady spot for the pram and join the
twins.

They got home in time for tea, nicely tired and went
happily to bed after they had talked to their mother on
the phone. There was no change in her mother's
condition, Mrs Burns told Deborah, and she asked if
everything was all right at home. Deborah said that
everything was fine, that the children had been as
good as gold and that Deirdre was a model baby, and
would Mrs Burns like to talk to Mary?

A diplomatic gesture which earned her a pleased
look, for Mary was delighted.

The next day followed the same pattern as the first,
pleasant but filled with the many chores which went
with three children. Deborah phoned her mother in
the evening, assured her that she was completely
happy and not in the least overworked and then went
to bed early. The children had been very good, she

thought sleepily as she curled up comfortably, and tomorrow there would be a respite because they were going to a friend's birthday party at the other end of the village. She would take them there, with Dee in the pram and then go back and have tea in the garden. Mary would be going to her wedding in the morning and once Mrs Twist had gone she would have the house to herself. Only for an hour or two but it would be a small pleasure to look forward to.

They had their dinner earlier than usual so that Mrs Twist could wash up the dishes before she went home. Deborah coaxed the children into fresh clothes, fed the baby and set off with her little party. There was a good deal of noise coming from the house as they approached it; the windows were wide open and there was a record player belting out the latest pop music. Deborah handed the twins over to a rather harassed woman at the door, promised to collect them at six o'clock, and went off with the pram and the sleeping Deirdre. Simon had muttered a gruff goodbye as they went, but Suzanne had flung her arms round Deborah's neck and hugged her.

It was a glorious day; Deborah strolled along admiring the view, talking from time to time to Deirdre who chuckled and crowed and then dropped off to sleep. She was still sleeping when Deborah reached the house unlocked the door and carried her inside to finish her nap in her cot.

It was early for tea, but the prospect of half an hour in the garden under the open window of the nursery was very tempting. Deborah crossed the hall to go to the kitchen and put on the kettle and presently took her tray on to the patio under the nursery window. She could have spent the rest of the day there but the twins had to be fetched and Deirdre put back into her pram. Deborah whisked round the kitchen, getting things ready for the twins' supper; she could feed the baby while they ate it. It was still pleasantly warm as she went unhurriedly through the village, collected the twins and walked them back smartly. They were over excited, over tired and peevish. The next hour or so tried her patience and her temper, but at last they were all sleeping and she took off her apron, pushed the hair back from her hot face and went downstairs. Mary wouldn't be back until late and she had a key, mused Deborah, her mind pleasantly occupied with supper and the thought of an early night with a book as she reached the hall and started towards the kitchen. She was half-way there when the bell pealed, quite gently and only once. Not Mary, she would have let herself in, not any of Mrs Burns' friends; they knew she was away—her husband? Deborah, who had a romantic mind, pictured him hot footing it half-way round the world to be with his wife and children as she went to the door and opened it.

Not Mrs Burns' husband; she had seen a wedding photo, he was dark and not much above middle-height and had a moustache, the man on the doorstep was twice as tall and wide. Well, even allowing for exaggeration he was a very large man and solid with it. Besides, he had iron grey hair, bright blue eyes and no moustache. She said enquiringly, 'Yes,' in a severe voice, while a host of unpleasant ideas about thieves and robbers and kidnappers seeped into her head.

'My God,' observed the man softly, 'I thought the species was extinct.' And when she looked nonplussed, 'Nannies,' he explained kindly, 'that's what you are, isn't it? I thought you worthy aproned ladies had been swallowed whole by the au pair girls.'

Not only probably a thief thought Deborah, a trifle

wildly, but also mentally unstable. 'Be good enough to go away,' she said in the firm no-nonsense voice she had been taught to use at the training college.

He leaned his elegantly clad person against the door frame and said equably: 'I haven't had a nanny for a long time; I never obeyed her anyway. I'm coming in.'

'You are not!' The two little terrors and baby Deirdre suddenly became very precious; he didn't know they were in the house, of course, but once inside he might go anywhere.

He changed his tactics. 'This is Peggy Burns' house?'

She nodded.

'Good, so I'll come in . . .'

'I don't know who you are,' she protested.

'I don't happen to have my birth certificate with me, would a passport do?' He was amused still but impatient now. 'You're alone in the house?'

She didn't answer and he tried again. 'Is Mrs Burns at home?'

'No.'

'Chatty little thing, aren't you? Where is she?'

Deborah was standing squarely in the doorway her small, rather plump person by no means filling it. 'At her mother's house.'

She watched his face change to become serious. 'Is she ill?'

'Her mother? Yes. Mrs Burns went yesterday—no the day before that. Now will you please go away?'

For answer she felt two large hands clasp her waist and she was lifted gently aside as he went past her and into the sitting room, where he picked up the phone. She closed the door and went after him, watching while he dialled a number, staring at the wall in front of him. He was a good looking man, in his mid-thirties perhaps. She wondered who he was; if he was an intruder she couldn't do much about it now, but he looked different suddenly, serious and worried, his voice was different too, no longer casual and so amused. He got the number and asked for Mrs Burns and then said: 'Peggy? what's wrong? I got back a couple of days early and came to see you. There's a small gorgon here, defending your children with her life's blood . . .'

He stood listening while Peggy talked. 'I'm coming over right away. No I didn't get your cable—I'd already left. I'll be with you in a couple of hours, maybe a good deal less.'

He listened again and turned to look at Deborah. 'Coping very well, I should have said; starched backbone and a mouth like a rat trap. I'd hate to be in her bad books.' And then 'Hang on love, I'll be with you in no time at all.'

He put the phone down. 'Any chance of a cup of coffee and a sandwich?' He smiled suddenly and she almost forgave him for calling her a gorgon, then she remembered the rat trap. 'Certainly Mr . . .' She gave him a steely look and he smiled again. 'Peggy's brother, Gideon Beaufort. And you?'

'Nanny,' said Deborah coldly and went away to the kitchen, where she made a pot of coffee and cut sandwiches, by now in a very nasty temper, not improved by his appearance through the door and the manner in which he wolfed the sandwiches as fast as she could cut them. She banged a mug and the coffee pot down in front of him, put milk and sugar within reach and said frostily: 'Excuse me, I'm going upstairs to the children.'

She crept into the night nursery and found them asleep, their small flushed faces looking angelic. She tucked in blankets, went to close one of the windows a little and let out a soundless squeak as a large hand came down on her shoulder. 'Nice, aren't they?' whispered their uncle. 'Little pests when they are awake of course.'

Deborah had got her breath back. 'I might have screamed,' she hissed almost soundlessly, 'frightening me like that, you should know better . . .' She glared up at him. 'I thought you were in a hurry to see your mother?'

He was serious again. 'I am, but I missed lunch and tea and jet lag was catching up on me. I'm going now. You're all right on your own?'

'Mary will be back later, thank you. Besides I have a definitely starched backbone and a mouth like a rat trap, haven't I? That should put the most hardened criminal off.'

'Did I say that? Next time we meet I'll apologise handsomely.'

They were in the hall, he gave her an encouraging pat on the shoulder and opened the door. He went without another word, not even goodbye. She heard a car start up outside but she didn't go to a window to see it. She never wanted to see the wretch again. Rude, arrogant, bent on scaring the hair off her head. She went to the dining room and gave herself a glass of sherry and then went round the house, locking the doors and shutting the windows. If anyone else rang the bell she had no intention of answering it. She got her supper, sitting over it reading a novel from the well-stocked bookshelves, and then fed Deirdre and settled her for the night. The twins were out cold, humped untidily in their beds. She tucked them in and dropped a kiss on their rosy cheeks and then went downstairs again to wait for Mary; somehow she didn't fancy going to bed until that lady was back.

Mary came home just after eleven o'clock. It had been a marvellous wedding, she told Deborah, the bride had looked beautiful and so had the bridesmaids; she didn't mention the bridegroom—a necessary but unnoticed cog in the matrimonial wheel. And lovely food she continued, accepting the coffee which Deborah thoughtfully put before her. The drink must have been lovely too; Mary was going to have a nasty head in the morning. It hardly seemed the time to tell her about Mr Beaufort, but Mary, revived by the hot drink, wanted to know what sort of a day she had had, and Deborah, skimming lightly over the gorgon and rat trap bits, told her.

'Such a nice gentleman,' observed Mary, still a bit muzzy, 'I've known him for a long time now, always so polite and so good with the children.'

She looked at Deborah and smiled and Deborah smiled back; she would hardly have described Mr Beaufort's manners as polite although she was fair enough to hold back her judgment on his avuncular affability. She gave Mary another cup of coffee and then urged her to her bed. However much they might want to sleep late in the morning, there would be no chance; the twins would see to that, and Deirdre, although a placid baby, was unlikely to forego her morning feed.

The twins, bursting with energy, made sure that Deborah was up early. There was no sign of Mary as Deborah made herself a cup of tea and debated whether to take one to the housekeeper, but decided to wait for another hour and feed Deirdre while the twins got themselves dressed. She thanked heaven for Deirdre's placid disposition as she washed unwilling faces and squeezed toothpaste out on to brushes; the baby was already asleep again which would give her time to give the twins their breakfast, and with any luck, allow her to bolt a slice of toast herself. By some miracle they were ready when Aunty Doris arrived; Deborah handed them over clean, well fed and with shining faces and nipped indoors again to take a cup of tea to Mary.

'I have a headache,' said Mary predictably.

'I brought you a couple of aspirin, if you take them now and lie still for ten minutes or so, it'll go. Do you fancy breakfast? I'm going to make some toast presently, after I've bathed Dee and put her into the pram. I'll make you a slice.'

They sat down together presently in the kitchen with Dee in her pram, banging a saucepan lid with a spoon. Rather hard on Mary.

Mrs Burns rang during the morning. Her mother was better, she told Deborah, and it had been wonderful to see her brother, 'So unexpected—I mean I'd sent him a cable—I couldn't phone because I wasn't quite sure where he was, but I didn't think he'd get here for a few days. He's been marvellous; seen the doctors and found another nurse so that I don't have to stay up at night and he's going to stay until Mother's well enough to go to a Nursing Home, and by then Bill should be home, so I don't have to worry. You're all right, Nanny, no problems?'

I have problems, thought Deborah, one of them is having a rat trap for a mouth, but out loud she said, with her usual calm, 'No, none, Mrs Burns. The children are splendid and Dee is such an easy baby.' Then added for good measure, 'And Mary is super.'

'Oh, good. Gideon seemed to think that you were managing very well. I think I'll be here for at least a week, perhaps a little longer than that. Will you manage until then? Get anything you need at the village stores, I've an account there. Oh, and will you ask Mary to send on some undies and another dress? The grey cotton jersey will do—I've almost nothing with me.'

Deborah hung up and handed the message on, reflecting that it must be nice to have people to do things for you; she suspected that Mrs Burns had always had that from the moment she was born and kindly fate had handed her a doting husband who carried on the good work. Probably the horrible brother was her slave too, although, upon reflection, she couldn't imagine him being anyone's slave.

She had no time to reflect for long, however, Mary's headache had gone but she was still lethargic so that Deborah found it prudent to do as much around the house as she could. At least dinner was almost ready by the time the twins were brought back, both in furious tears and looking as though their clothes hadn't been changed for a couple of weeks. 'They had a little upset,' explained Aunty Doris with false sweetness, 'they're such lively little people.'

There was nothing for it but to be patient and put them into the bath, wheedle them into clean clothes and lastly load the washing machine once more, before sitting them down to a delayed dinner which they stubbornly refused to eat.

But after a long walk in the afternoon they cheered up, ate a splendid tea and went to their beds, looking too good to be true.

By the end of the next two days they had accepted Deborah as a great friend, a firm friend who didn't allow them to have their own way, but who nevertheless was good fun. The days had settled into a routine, a rather dull one for Deborah but busy with washing and ironing and feeding and keeping the twins happy and amused. It was at the end of the first week when the twins, bored with being indoors all the morning because of the rain, started playing up. Providentially, the rain stopped after their dinner and, although it was still damp underfoot, Deborah stuffed small feet into wellies, tucked Dee snugly into her pram and went into the garden. There was a good sized lawn behind the house. She put the pram in a patch of watery sunshine, made sure that the baby was asleep and fetched a ball. But half an hour of kicking that around wasn't enough for the twins, they demanded something else for a change. Deborah caught them in either hand and began to prance up and down the grass singing 'Here we come gathering nuts in May' and had them singing too, dancing to and fro with her.

Deborah didn't know what made her turn her head. Gideon Beaufort was leaning on the patio rail, watching them, and even at that distance she took instant exception to the smile on his face.

CHAPTER TWO

DEBORAH stopped her singing and prancing so abruptly that the twins almost fell over. 'Good afternoon, Mr Beaufort,' she said in a cold way which was almost wholly swamped by the twins' ecstatic shrieks, although half-way across the grass Simon turned to shout: 'He's not a mister, he's a professor,' before flinging himself at his uncle.

'Very clearly put,' observed the professor, disentangling himself slowly. 'Now you can do the same for me and introduce Nanny.'

His nephew eyed him with impatience. 'Well, she's just Nanny . . .'

'No name?'

He looked at Deborah and she said unwillingly: 'Farley—Deborah Farley.'

'Charming—a popular name with the Puritans, I believe.' His voice was so bland that she decided to let that pass.

'What's a puritan?' asked Suzy.

'A sober person who thought it wrong to sing and dance and be happy.'

'Nanny's not one,' declared his niece. 'We've been singing and dancing,' she explained earnestly.

The professor nodded. 'Yes, and very nicely too.' He smiled at Deborah who gave him a cool look; the gorgon's rat trap still rankled.

'Is Mummy coming?' demanded Simon.

'Not today old fellow—Granny's better but not quite well yet. I thought I'd drop in and see how

24

things are.' He strolled over to the pram and peered inside. 'Dee's asleep—I've never seen such a child for dozing off.' He glanced at Deborah. 'She must be very easy to look after.'

'No trouble at all,' agreed Deborah airily.

'In that case perhaps I might stay for tea without straining your work load too much?' He smiled again with such charm that she only just stopped in time from smiling back in return.

'Certainly, Professor, the children will be delighted, won't you, my dears? Mary did some baking this morning, so there'll be a cake.'

Mary's welcome was warm and seemed even warmer by reason of Deborah's brisk efficiency. She wheeled the pram under the nursery window so that she might hear if Dee wakened; removed the twins to be tidied and washed for tea, sat them down at the table, one on each side of their uncle, and went to help carry in the tea tray, the plate of bread and butter and the cake Mary had so providentially baked.

The tea tray was taken from her as she entered the nursery by a disarmingly polite professor. What was more he remained so throughout the meal, talking nothings to her when not engaged in answering the twins' ceaseless questions. Deborah felt a certain reluctance when it was time to feed Deirdre, but she got up from the table, excused herself politely, cautioned the twins to behave and made to leave the room. At the door she hesitated: 'I get Dee ready for bed once she's been fed,' she explained, 'so I'll wish you goodbye, Professor, please tell Mrs Burns that everything is just as it should be.'

'Oh, I'm staying the night. Did I not tell you? I'm so sorry.' He sounded all concern, but all the same she knew that he was laughing silently. 'Mary said that she would get a room ready for me.' He added silkily: 'You don't mind?'

'I, mind? Certainly not. It is none of my business, Professor Beaufort. I daresay you've also asked Mary to cook extra . . .'

'No,' he told her gently, 'she suggested it. Should I have asked you?'

Deborah went pink; on the whole she was a good tempered girl but today her good nature was being tried severely; besides she had been rude.

'I'm only in charge of the children,' she told him, 'Mary runs the house. Besides I'm only temporary.'

As she dealt with the small Dee's needs, she could hear the twins giggling and shouting and the occasional rumble of their uncle's voice. 'They'll be quite out of hand—I'll never get them to bed,' she observed to the placid infant on her knee. 'He'll get them all worked up . . .'

But surprisingly, when she went to fetch the twins for their baths and bed, they went with her like lambs. Not so much as a peep out of them and so unnaturally good that Deborah wondered if they were sickening for something. She put a small capable hand on their foreheads and found them reassuringly cool and finally demanded to know what was the matter with them.

They exchanged glances and looked at her with round blue eyes, 'Uncle Gideon made us promise so we won't tell. Are we being good?'

'Yes—and I can't think why.' She gave them a close look. 'You're not up to mischief, are you?'

Meekly they assured her that they weren't. She tucked them into their beds, kissed them goodnight, and went to her room, where she did her face carefully, scraped her sandy hair back into a severe style becoming to a well-trained nanny, and went downstairs.

Professor Beaufort was stretched out on one of the outsize sofas in the sitting room, his eyes closed. She stood and looked at him; he was very good looking she conceded, and like that, asleep, he was nice; it was when he stared at her with bright blue eyes and spoke to her in that bland voice that she disliked him. She gave a faint yelp when he spoke.

'You don't look in the least like a nanny should.' He observed and got to his feet in one swift movement, to tower over her, beaming.

She fought against his charm; saying severely: 'I assure you that I am fully qualified.'

'Oh, I can see that, you handle the twins like a veteran. Tell me—what is your ambition? To get a post with some blue-blooded family and stay with them all your life and then retire to an estate cottage?'

She felt rage bubble inside her. 'I might possibly marry,' she pointed out sweetly and choked at his bland: 'He will be a brave man ... Shall we have a drink? Mary told me that dinner would be ready in ten minutes or so.'

She accepted a sherry and wished that she had asked for something dashing like whisky or even gin and tonic. Just so that he would see that she wasn't the prim, dedicated nanny that he had decided she was. But she did the next best thing; she asked for a second drink and he poured it without comment, only his eyebrows lifted in an amused arc which she didn't see. She tossed it off smartly so that she was able to face their tête à tête meal with equanimity and a chattiness quite unlike her usual quiet manner.

Professor Beaufort quite shamelessly led her on, his grave face offering no hint of his amusement. She told him about her three brothers, her home in Dorchester, cousin Rachel and only just stopped herself in time from regaling him with some of the foibles she had had to put up with from various parents whose children she had taken care of. Finally, vaguely aware that she was talking too much, she asked: 'And is your work very interesting, Professor? I'm not quite sure what you do . . .'

He passed his plate for a second helping of Mary's delicious apple pie. 'I study the production and distribution of money and goods.'

'Yes, but don't you work?'

'Er—yes. I have an office and I travel a good deal as well as lecturing regularly.'

'Oh—do people want to know—about money and goods, I mean?'

'It helps if they do. The management of public affairs, the disposition of affairs of state or government departments, the judicious use of public money—someone has to know about such things.'

'And do you?' she queried.

'One might say that I have a basic knowledge . . .'

'It sounds dull. I'd rather have the children,' said Deborah, still rather lively from the sherry.

He said slowly: 'I think that possibly you are right, Nanny. I hadn't given the matter much thought, but now that you mention it, I shall look into it. Do you suppose that Mary would give us our coffee on the patio? It's a delightful evening.'

Somehow being called 'Nanny' brought her down to earth with a bump. She poured their coffee almost in silence and when she had drunk hers excused herself with the plea that Dee would be waking for her feed very shortly. She wished him goodnight, every inch the children's nurse, and went upstairs. It was too early to feed Dee; she pottered round her room for half an hour, aware that she would have liked to have stayed and talked, and aware too that she had said too much anyway.

She gave the baby her bottle presently, turned the twins up the right way and tucked them in once more, and got herself ready for bed. It was very warm and she had taken too hot a bath; she sat by the open window for quite some time, brushing her hair and thinking about her future. The professor had been joking, supposing her to be content with a lifelong job with the same family and an old age in some cottage, but it held more than a grain of truth. She didn't relish the idea in the least. She got up and went to look at herself in the triple mirror. No one—no man—was likely to fall for her; sandy hair was bad enough, sandy eyelashes were the utter end; the lovely green eyes she ignored and studied the rest of her face; the small straight nose and much too wide mouth above a determined chin; there was nothing there to enchant a man. She overlooked the fact that she had a pretty figure and nice hands and legs, all she could think of was curly blonde hair and bright blue eyes fringed by dark curling lashes. Her own lashes curled, but being sandy they were almost invisible. 'I could of course dye them,' she told her image, but perhaps that would make the rest of her face look odd. She got into bed, fretting about the eyelashes and fell asleep almost at once.

She awoke to pitch darkness and a whimper, thin as a kitten's protest; by the time she was sitting up in bed to listen, the whimper had become a furious roar. One of the twins was having a nightmare; she shot out of bed and went on bare feet through the day nursery and into the adjoining room where the pair of them slept. It was Suzanne, half awake and bellowing with fright. Deborah plucked her gently from her bed, gathered her into her arms and sat down in the little arm chair by the window, half strangled by the child's arms. It took a few moments to wake her up completely and twice as long to get her to stop crying. Deborah had soothed the sobbing to a series of sniffs and gulps when Simon woke, sat up in bed and demanded to know why Suzy was crying. The two of them were very close; he got out of his bed and came to join them, perching on the arm of the chair, demanding to know in a loud voice what the matter was.

'Well, that's what we are going to find out,' said Deborah reasonably, 'I expect it was a nasty dream, wasn't it? But you are wide awake now and dreams aren't real you know. You shall tell me about it and then you'll forget it and when you've had a nice drink of warm milk, you'll go to sleep again and wake up in the morning quite happy again. Now tell Nanny what made you cry, darling?'

Simon slid off the chair and she turned her head to see why. The professor was leaning in the doorway, huge and magnificent in a dazzlingly-striped dressing-gown. The little boy hurled himself at him and was swung into his arms, to be carried to his bed and sat on his uncle's knee.

Deborah, her hair hanging in a clean, shining curtain on her shoulders and down her back, bare feet digging into the thick rug, gave the professor a passing glance, and turned her attention to Suzy; she had forgotten that she hadn't bothered to put on her dressing-gown and there was nothing in his face to remind her of that fact. She bent her head to hear the child's tearful whispering, tossing back her sandy tresses with an impatient hand. The telling took some time with a good deal of sniffing and gulping but she listened patiently and finally when the child had come to a halt said hearteningly: 'There now—it's all right again, isn't it? You've told us all about it and although it was a nasty dream, you've forgotten it because we all know about it, don't we? Now I'm going to get you some milk and then I'll sit here until you've gone to sleep again . . .'

'Let me have her here,' suggested the professor, who went on: 'I should put your dressing-gown on before you go downstairs.' His voice was quite impersonal but she gave a horrified squeak and pattered out of the room without another word. Bundled into her useful saxe-blue robe, buttoned from neck to ankle, she was glad of the few minutes it took in which to heat the milk. What must he have thought? She was no prude, after all she had three brothers, but children's nurses to the best of her knowledge didn't go prancing round in the dead of night in cotton nighties and nothing else when there were strangers around. And the professor was a stranger, and although she didn't care a jot for his opinion of her, she squirmed at the idea of giving him something to snigger about . . . snigger wasn't the right word, she conceded, give him his due, he wasn't like that. All the same she dared say that he would have no hesitation in remarking on her dishabille if he felt like it.

She removed the milk from the Aga, poured it into two mugs, put them on a tray and bore it upstairs with a stiff dignity which caused the professor's fine mouth to twitch, although he said nothing, merely took the mug she offered Simon while she sat Suzy on her lap and coaxed her to drink. The pair of them were sleepy now; the milk finished, she tucked them back into bed, refused the professor's offer to sit with them until they were well and truly asleep and bade him a dismissive goodnight. Only he wouldn't be dismissed. 'I'm going to make us a hot drink,' he informed her, 'I'll be in the kitchen when you are ready.'

He cast an eye over the two drowsy children. 'Ten minutes at the outside, I should imagine.'

'I don't want . . .' began Deborah and was stopped by the steely look he bent upon her. 'You will have to be up soon after six o'clock for Dee—it is now a little after two in the morning; you will need to sleep as quickly as possible, a hot drink helps.'

He was right, of course, although it wouldn't be the first time she had gone short of sleep, and he was right about the twins too, they were asleep within minutes of being tucked in. She waited for a good five minutes and then went downstairs to the kitchen, cosy and magnificently equipped, to find the professor pouring steaming milk into two mugs.

'Cocoa,' he said, barely glancing at her, and handed her one.

She sat down at the table and drank it as obediently as Suzy had done, and tried to think of something to say; but small talk didn't come easily at the dead of night and anyway, her companion seemed unworried by the silence. She had almost finished when he observed: 'It's the twins' birthday in two weeks' time— I'm giving them a dog—a golden labrador puppy— he'll keep them busy and sleep in their room, that should stop the nightmares.'

'You approve of animals in bedrooms?'

He gave her a surprised look and then smiled thinly. 'I suppose you have been trained to discourage it?'

'Well yes, but personally I think there's no harm in it. Our cat always sleeps on my bed when I'm at home.' She drank the last of her cocoa. 'We haven't got a dog—at least he died last year . . . I don't suppose you have much time for one?'

'Very little, but I have three. Two labradors and a Jack Russell—there are cats too—my housekeeper has two and a constant supply of kittens.' He put down his mug. 'You had better go to bed Nanny.'

He had spoken so abruptly that she opened her green eyes wide, just for only a few moments she had forgotten that he didn't much like her. She put her cup in the sink, said 'Goodnight' in a quiet little voice and went back upstairs. The twins were sound asleep, so was Dee; she got into bed and was asleep within two minutes.

She had fed Dee and was dressed and ready for her day before the twins woke, their disturbed night forgotten and bounding with energy, but she was used to them by now; they were sitting down to their breakfast no more than five minutes late, shovelling corn flakes into their small mouths by the time their uncle appeared, Mary hard on his heels with fresh coffee and toast. He bade the room a general good-morning, gave it as his intention to drive the twins to school and ate a huge breakfast with no more than a quick look at Deborah, sitting behind the coffee pot, clean and starched and severe. 'In that case,' she remarked, 'I'd better phone Aunty Doris and ask her not to come.'

'For God's sake, do—that garrulous woman . . .'

'Little pitchers have long ears,' said Deborah sternly and then blushed because she had sounded like a prig.

'What's a pitcher?' asked Suzy.

'Doesn't God like Aunty Doris?' asked Simon.

'You see what you've done?' snapped Deborah and was answered by a great bellow of laughter.

The house seemed very quiet after they had gone,

the three of them. Deborah bathed and dressed Dee
and put her out in the garden in the pram before
racing round making beds and tidying up.

'It'll be a nice roast chicken for lunch,' said Mary.
'Mister Gideon says he must go this afternoon—he's
partial to my trifle too.'

Deborah tried to think of something suitable to say
to this; it was evident that Mary doted on the man and
there was no point in offending the dear soul by saying
what she thought about the professor; after all, she
was unlikely to meet him again. She would forget him,
just as she had forgotten a number of people she had
met and disliked during the last few years.

Mary was looking at her, waiting for her to make
some comment. She said brightly: 'I'm sure he'll love
that—men like sweet things, don't they?'

The housekeeper gave a rich chuckle. 'That they
do—never grow up, they don't, not in some ways. Now
Mr Burns, he likes a nice chocolate pudding.'

She watched Deborah collect an armful of small
garments ready for the washing machine, and added
comfortably: 'Well, I'll be off to my kitchen. I must
say you're a real help around the house, Nanny, not
like some of those toffee-nosed au pairs Mrs Burns has
tried out. Not a success they weren't.'

Deborah looked up briefly. 'I'm only here for a
short time, Mary. I expect Mrs Burns will have other
plans.'

'Ah, well as long as they speak English,' she sighed.

The professor appeared suddenly and almost
silently, just as Deborah was settling Dee back in her
pram after her morning feed. 'Any coffee?' he wanted
to know.

'Mary will have it ready, I expect.' Deborah kicked
the brake off, and began to wheel the pram across the

lawn towards the drive. She usually had her coffee with Mary, this morning she would go for a walk first and leave the housekeeper to enjoy their visitor's company.

But it seemed that the professor had other ideas. He laid a large hand on the pram's handle so that she was forced to stop. He said smoothly: 'You don't have to run away you know, I don't bite; we've had no chance to get to know each other.'

'What would be the point?' she wanted to know matter-of-factly. 'We're most unlikely to meet again; I go all over the place.'

He had steered the pram towards the patio, anchored it there and put his head through the open french window to shout to Mary. When he emerged he observed in a friendly way: 'You must see quite a lot of life,' and spoilt it by adding: 'From the wings as it were.'

She said in a decidedly acid voice: 'I daresay that's more fun than being buried alive in economics.'

'Ah, but when I've reduced high powered chaos to orderly statistics, I er—I enjoy myself.'

Mary came with the coffee and the three of them sat drinking it in the bright sunshine while the talk eddied to and fro between Mary and the professor, with Deborah not saying much. She was in truth, very occupied in wondering just how he enjoyed himself. In a room full of computers, perhaps? catching up on a little light reading in the Financial Times? entertaining some pretty girl to dinner, spending the evening—the night, with her? more than likely.

'A penny for them,' said the professor suddenly so that she went a bright and becoming pink. She mumbled something and Mary said comfortably: 'Thinking about where she'll go next, I'll be bound.

Isn't that right, Nanny? For all you know it'll be one
of those Arab countries with gold bath taps and a
horde of servants—much in demand our nannies are in
that part of the world. Would you love to go there,
dear?'

'No, I don't think so.' It was a great relief that she
hadn't had to answer Professor Beaufort's question.

'But you do travel?'

'Well, yes, but I've only been to the south of France
and Brussels and Scotland. I'm quite happy to stay in
England.'

'But you don't object to going abroad?' The
professor's voice was very casual.

'Not in the least. Children are the same anywhere.'
She put down her coffee cup and got to her feet. 'I'll
take Dee for her walk.' She glanced at her watch, but
before she could speak: 'I'll fetch the twins, Nanny.
Mary, may we have lunch just a little early so that I
can get away in good time?'

As she wheeled the pram away Deborah took time
to tell herself how pleasant it would be when he'd
gone—quite quiet and a bit dull perhaps, but pleasant;
he was a disturbing person to have around the house.
'He may be your uncle,' she told the sleeping Dee,
'but I don't like him. Him and his economics, indeed.'
She tossed her sandy head and marched smartly
through the village and up the hill on the other side
where presently she sat down with her back against a
tree until it was time to go back and give Dee her
orange juice.

Lunch was a boisterous affair which petered out
into tears and tantrums from the twins because their
uncle was going away again.

He swung them in the air in turn and hugged them
briefly. 'If you are very good and don't howl in that

frightful fashion and do exactly what Nanny tells you and eat your dinners without fuss, I'll give you each a real bicycle. It had better be before Christmas otherwise I might get in Father Christmas's way. Let's see, shall we say the first of December?'

He left them with a brief nod to Deborah and a much warmer leave taking from Mary. If she hadn't been kept so busy all the afternoon counting days on the calendar for the twins' benefit, she might have had the time to feel annoyed about that. Although in all fairness she herself had pointed out that they were most unlikely to see each other again, and as far as she could see they had absolutely nothing in common.

There was no point in thinking about him; she dismissed him from her mind and bent to the task of keeping the twins occupied in a suitable fashion, making sure that they ate their food and acting as mediator when they quarrelled—which was often. What with the pair of them and baby Dee, who although no trouble at all, needed her attentions more or less round the clock, the next few days passed rapidly enough. But Mrs Burns gave no indication as to when she would return although she telephoned each day.

It was four days since the professor had left, just as they were about to start a picnic tea on the lawn, that Mrs Burn's racy sports car turned into the drive and stopped with a squealing of brakes before her front door.

The children had seen of course, and were already racing to meet her as she got out of the car. They closed in on her and for a moment there was pandemonium; laughing and shrieks of delight and Mrs Burns explaining that she had come home, Granny was well enough to leave and Daddy was on his way back too. She crossed the lawn to where Deborah sat with Dee on her lap, beginning to explain all over again long before she reached her.

'I should have phoned, Nanny, but I wanted to make sure that Doctor Wyatt was perfectly satisfied with my mother's progress. There's a nurse with her of course, but when he said that she was quite out of danger and that I need stay no longer, I just threw my things into a bag and came racing home. And Bill's on his way back too; it's all so exciting!'

She held out her arms for the baby who smiled contentedly showing a good deal of gum. Her mother kissed the top of her head: 'They all look marvellous. Have they been good? I know you said each day that they were giving no trouble, but I daresay you were driven out of your mind . . .'

Deborah laughed. 'No, indeed, I wasn't—and they were good, really they were. Would you like tea here, or indoors?' She got to her feet. 'I'll go and tell Mary . . .'

'No need, Nanny. I'm going to have tea here with you. I'll borrow Simon's mug and he can share with Suzy.' She settled gracefully on the garden seat and patted it. 'Come and sit beside me and tell me what you think of my family.' She tucked Dee under her arm, told the twins to sit on the grass beside her, and watched Deborah pouring the tea, handing round mugs of milk and plates of bread and butter.

'Gideon came?' she said and there was a question behind the remark. 'Yes,' said Deborah equably, 'The twins loved it—he took them to school . . .'

'God doesn't like Aunty Doris,' shrilled Simon.

Mrs Burns said calmly: 'I suspect you've got it wrong, darling; Uncle Gideon's been using grown up language and it doesn't quite mean the same as the things we talk about.'

'Nanny frowned at him . . .'

Mrs Burns looked at Deborah. 'He may be a professor, but he has his lighter moments—he can be very tiresome—I'm always telling him so, aren't I, darlings?'

With no effect at all, thought Deborah.

Later, with the children in bed, over dinner with Mrs Burns Deborah gave a blow by blow account of her days. 'So you see, they've been very good, and great fun too.'

'Splendid. Don't go rushing off, will you?' Mrs Burns turned persuasive eyes on to Deborah. 'Bill will be home late tomorrow; the children will go berserk, they always do, and they'll need someone to make them eat and go to bed and so on, so please stay for a little longer—unless you've another job waiting?'

'Well, I haven't actually—and of course I'll stay until you don't need me.'

'Oh, good! What a relief. My mother wants to see the children, I thought we might drive over after Bill gets home and let her see them for a few minutes. She dotes on them and it'll do her good.'

Mrs Burns suddenly looked very young and sad. 'Oh, Nanny I was so frightened. I thought Mother wasn't going to get better. Thank heaven Gideon came, he's so sensible and always knows what to do, just like Bill, I mean he'd got everything organised within an hour of his getting there and he was so sure that Mother was going to get better that I believed him—he was calm and certain about it. He is such a dear, don't you agree?'

'He's a marvellous uncle,' said Deborah guardedly and Mrs Burns looked at her, a flicker of amusement in her eyes although she didn't say anything.

It was difficult to keep the children even moderately

quiet the next day, by the time their father arrived
they were in bed, wide awake, and since it was quite
obvious that they had no intention of going to sleep
until he had got home, Deborah sat between their
beds, reading soothingly from Little Grey Rabbit and
very relieved when at last they heard a car turn into
the drive and stop before the house. There was no
holding the twins; she got them into their dressing
gowns, thrust wriggling impatient feet into slippers
and led them downstairs. They broke free of her
restraining hands once they reached the hall and flung
themselves at their father standing in the drawing
room doorway. Deborah waited where she was, not
sure what to do; the children should have been in their
beds, on the other hand they hadn't seen their father
for some weeks and from the look of it, he was
delighted to see them again. He scooped them up and
swung them round laughing and turned to smile at his
wife. They all looked so happy that Deborah felt a
pang of loneliness, instantly forgotten when Mrs
Burns caught sight of her and said: 'Bill, here's
Nanny, she's been marvellous—I don't know what I
would have done without her—and she's promised to
stay a little longer.'

Mr Burns smiled across at her. 'Hullo Nanny—I'm
glad to meet you and very grateful too. Once we've got
these little horrors in bed again, come down and have
a drink.'

Deborah was on the point of making some excuse,
but Mrs Burns said: 'Yes, do—I know you've had the
hell of a day with the children, but just come for a
little while, please.'

It was surprisingly easy to get the twins to bed now
that they were satisfied that their father was really
home; they were asleep at once and it wasn't quite

time for Dee's last feed. Deborah tidied her hair, powdered her flushed and rather tired face and went downstairs.

Mr Burns was sitting in an armchair, his wife perched beside him but he got up as Deborah went into the room, offered her sherry and poured it, and then waved her to a chair. 'I can't tell you what a relief· it was to hear how well you've been coping—Gideon sent me a most reassuring cable—it made all the difference, I can tell you—all those miles away and unable to get home to poor Peggy. We thought we might go over to Bath tomorrow—we'll take the children of course and if you would come too . . .?'

'Of course,' said Deborah in a quiet voice.

'Good, just a brief visit, you know. I'm very fond of my mother-in-law,' he smiled at his wife as he spoke, 'I'm glad and relieved that she's recovered. She wants to see the children and I want to see her, so if you could take charge of them for half an hour? There's a nice garden there—Dee can stay in her Moses basket.'

He was quite different from the professor, thought Deborah, listening to him; unassuming and reserved with a nice open face and kind eyes. 'We'll be quite all right, Mr Burns,' she assured him: 'Dee's such a good baby and I'll take something to amuse the twins. Shall we be going in the morning or later in the day?'

'An early lunch?' suggested Mr Burns to his wife and she nodded. 'We can have tea there, and be back in good time for the twins to be put to bed.'

Deborah put down her glass and stood up. 'It's time for Dee's feed. Thank you for my drink, goodnight Mrs Burns, goodnight Mr Burns.'

The twins naturally enough were enchanted at the idea of going to see Granny in Daddy's car, but they were still more delighted to hear that since lunch was to be early they wouldn't be going to school. Deborah took them for a walk; protesting loudly, rebellious hands holding on to the pram as she wheeled Dee off for the morning airing. 'Just for an hour,' coaxed Deborah. 'So that your father can get the car ready for this afternoon.'

They travelled in Mr Burns' estate car, roomy enough to take them all with the twins strapped into their seats and Deborah sitting between them with Dee on her lap. The weather was warm and sunny although the trees were showing the first early signs of autumn, although she was kept much too occupied to look around her.

Mrs Burns' mother lived in a nice old house a mile or two outside Bath and when they arrived Mrs Burns went in alone to make sure that her mother was feeling up to seeing them, then her husband joined her, leaving Deborah in the garden with the twins and Dee in her carry-cot. Luckily not for long, for they were impatient to see the invalid, and under dire threat not to so much as raise their voices, they were led inside with Deborah, Dee tucked under her arm, bringing up the rear.

Mrs Burns' mother was an elderly edition of her daughter and although she looked ill, she was still pretty in a faded way, but her eyes were bright and missed nothing. She was kissed carefully by the twins, admired Dee, and then turned her attention to Deborah. Not that she said much, but Deborah had the distinct impression that she was being closely examined, although she couldn't think why. If she could have stayed behind instead of taking the children back into the garden she would have found out . . .

'She'll do very well,' said Mrs Beaufort. 'Have you said anything?'

'Nothing, Mother—we thought we'd see what you thought, first, after all, you'll see quite a lot of her for several weeks.' She added, 'Bill likes her . . .'

'And Gideon,' said her mother. 'Which surprised me very much—you know what he's like and she's hardly his type. He says she unnerves him—probably all that sandy hair and those eyes. They are absolutely beautiful.'

'She's super with the kids.' Mrs Burns stooped to kiss her parent. 'Bill will talk to her tomorrow and get things settled. The doctors say another two weeks before you are fit to travel, that gives us time to get organised. Is Eleanor coming too?'

'Yes,' Mrs Beaufort was looking tired but interested. 'But for some reason best known to him, Gideon asks us not to mention that.'

She and her daughter stared at each other for a long moment. 'You don't say,' observed Mrs Burns, and then: 'We'll see, won't we?'

Deborah was under the trees at the end of the garden, making daisy chains for the twins while Dee slept. She would have liked a cup of tea and as if in answer to her thought, a stout woman came out of the house with a tray, and a moment or two later Mr and Mrs Burns came out too. They picnicked at leisure and presently Mr Burns carried the tray back indoors and they all got into the car once more and drove home. The children were sleepy by now and Deborah had a chance to mull over the afternoon; it was strange but she was unable to rid herself of the feeling that she had been on some sort of trial; perhaps they would tell her that she wasn't needed any more. It seemed more than likely when Mr Burns said over his shoulder as they stopped before the door: 'Nanny, I'd like to talk to you sometime. Tomorrow? Or perhaps this evening when you have some time to yourself?' He smiled at her kindly. 'After dinner if that suits you.'

She agreed calmly, already composing a letter to the agency in her head as she bore Dee off to the nursery and bedtime.

CHAPTER THREE

DEBORAH had imagined that she would be summoned to the study during the evening, but the three of them had dinner without any mention of the talk Mr Burns had suggested, it was only after they had had their coffee in the drawing room that he glanced at his wife and said: 'We should like to talk to you, Nanny. We hope that you haven't another job lined up because we would be very glad if you could come with us on holiday in a couple of weeks' time. We plan to take Mrs Beaufort away—a villa in the Algarve—where she can laze around in the sun and get really well again. Of course we shall take the children with us and we hope that you will come too. Three weeks or a month, and in the meantime if you would like to go home? Now that I am here, we can cope with the twins for a couple of weeks, but without you on holiday with us, I don't think that we could manage. Will you think about it and let us know? It won't be much of a holiday for you although we'll see that you get time to have to yourself each day . . .'

'We would be back in England about the end of October?' asked Deborah.

'Yes, but I can't give you the exact dates just yet.'

Deborah sounded matter-of-fact, but she was excited too. She liked the twins and Dee; compared with some of the children she had cared for, they were like angels. Besides, even though she would have her hands full all day, it would make a pleasant change. She didn't give herself time to weigh the pros and cons; she said in her calm way: 'Yes, I'll come with you, Mr Burns. I should like to go home first as you suggest, but I can be ready whenever you want. I've nothing in view at the moment, and I only have to let the agency know.'

'That calls for another drink,' declared Mr Burns and presently, nicely glowing from a second sherry, Deborah went up to bed. She didn't go to sleep at once; her usually sensible head was full of pleasant, excited thoughts. New clothes, suitable for the undoubtedly warm weather they would enjoy, a respite from going back to the agency and deciding which job she would take, there were usually several to choose from, and few of them so far, had been even bordering on perfection. Besides she had to admit to a feeling of faint discontent, not at all her usual self and as far as she could discover it came for no reason at all. She lay pondering this and since she couldn't find an answer, sensibly went to sleep.

She went home three days later, with the twins screaming goodbyes and come back soons at her, and with strict instructions to prepare herself for the journey. They were to travel in ten days' time, flying from Bristol they would then stay in the villa Mr Burns had hired for three weeks. She was to go to Bristol Airport and meet them there not later than ten o'clock in the morning. Mr Burns drove her home, staying briefly to have coffee with her mother before he went again.

'Such a nice man,' observed Mrs Farley, 'everything's turned out very nicely hasn't it darling? Let me see, it's almost the end of September, you'll be back home at the end of October, if you could get a temporary job until just before Christmas ... then in the New Year you could find a nice permanent post!'

'Yes, Mother,' agreed Deborah, with no desire at all to do any such thing. She would have to, of course, a girl had to be independent, her brothers were costing a lot and, although she was barely twenty-three, no one had asked her to marry. She had friends enough, cheerful young men who called her Debby, poured out their problems about girl friends into her sympathetic ear and teased her in a kindly, offhand way. They all liked her, indeed, were fond of her, but not one of them had had the idea of marrying her. And why should they, she would tell her reflection as she wound her sandy hair into a tidy coil, she had no looks to speak of. All the same it would be nice to have a proposal . . .

The faint, unsettled feeling was partly drowned in the fun of buying clothes; a couple of pretty cotton dresses, some skirts and tops, sandals and a swim suit and bikinis. No uniform, Mrs Burns had said, they so wanted to be in sun dresses or swim suits all day; even though she would be looking after the children, Deborah felt as though she was going on holiday. She packed with her usual neatness and wearing a sensible uncrushable two-piece, short sleeved, round necked and easy on the eye, she got into the car very early in the morning and settled herself beside her father, who hadn't needed much persuading to take a day off from the Bank and drive her to the Airport. It was a glorious morning with a faint autumnal chill which would presently give way to the sun's warmth. 'You'll come back as brown as a coffee bean,' declared her father.

'I go red, Father, and get covered in freckles—I shall have to wear a sun hat. I've packed lashings of Ambre Solaire though.'

'As long as you enjoy yourself, my dear.'

They had half an hour to spare at the airport, they drank a quick cup of coffee and then went to the reception area to look for the Burns family. They were already there, the twins sternly controlled by their father, Mrs Burns carrying Dee and Mrs Beaufort in a wheel chair. They all looked a little gloomy, but when they saw Deborah the gloom lifted as if by magic.

'Thank God!' said Mr Burns, and meant it. 'We should have fetched you over yesterday—we bit off rather more than we could chew. Still we're here now.' He beamed at her, shook hands with Mr Farley and edged away so that they might say goodbye. Mr Farley didn't linger, Deborah was a sensible girl, quite able to cope with any situation and quite unruffled. He turned to wave once and she waved back and then took Dee under one arm, attached the twins (holding hands) to her free hand and watched while Mrs Burns picked up her overnight bag and Mr Burns gave orders about the luggage before leading the little party briskly to the end of the reception hall. It didn't seem to be the same direction as everyone else was going but Mrs Burns and her mother, still in the chair being pushed by an airport attendant, looked quite unworried. Deborah, trailing the twins, brought up the rear.

It took her a minute or two to realise that they were flying by charter plane. A sensible, if expensive way of getting an invalid lady, two boisterous children and a baby, not to mention the Burns and herself, to their destination. They embarked smoothly, with Deborah settled between the twins and with Dee on her lap; Mrs Beaufort on her own now, stretched out on the opposite seat; and the Burns sitting in front. The twins were ominously quiet, Deborah gave them each a book to look at, saw with relief that Dee had dropped off, and prayed silently for at least half an hour's peace.

The children took no notice of take-off, immersed in their picture books they flicked over the pages with the blasé air of big businessmen flying the Atlantic for the hundredth time. Deborah, anxious not to disturb the peace, sat quietly; she didn't care for flying, but since her work took her among people who accepted it as a matter of course, she accepted it too. All the same, she was glad when they were airborne.

The unnatural quiet came to an end, of course, Deborah handed out drinks and biscuits, played endless games designed to keep the children in their seats, fed Dee and then handed her over to a refreshed Mrs Burns while she had a drink herself. Mrs Beaufort had gone to sleep and Deborah envied her; it was by far the best way to fly she considered; wiping sticky little fingers, changing Dee and settling her to sleep again, beginning an endless story which lasted until they touched down at Faro Airport.

There were two cars waiting for them, a large estate car and a small Fiat. Deborah, the children, the luggage and Mr Burns travelled in the first, Mrs Burns followed them with her mother comfortably installed in the back of the Fiat. The party took some time to get settled and it was by now the hottest part of the day and they had an hour's drive before them; but so far everything had gone smoothly and the clear blue sky and the sunshine gave promise of pleasant times ahead. As an added bonus the twins fell asleep as soon as they started, curled up against Deborah. What with their small warm bodies pressed to hers, and Dee on her lap, she grew hot and rather sticky. Probably her nose was shining and her hair a mess but at least her dress looked fresh and cool. She sat very still, and since Mr Burns spoke only occasionally, admired the scenery.

There were mountains in the distance, tree covered, sweeping down to orange groves and vineyards and fields of stunted olive trees, and every few miles a village—a narrow street lined with small square houses with shuttered windows and when a door was open she could glimpse inside, black emptiness. Of course, there would be furniture there and people, but they weren't visible. There were dogs too, lying round in the dust, taking no notice of anyone, sensibly asleep like everyone else. The sea was on their left but it was some miles away although there were frequent signposts pointing seawards, but for the moment Deborah was quite content to marvel at the oranges and lemons and the brilliance of the flowers. There was a good deal of traffic on the road, but they travelled fast, Mr Burns explaining over one shoulder that once they had arrived everyone must have a rest before unpacking. Deborah agreed cheerfully, well aware that the twins, refreshed by their nap, would want to be up and doing, and since she had been hired as their nanny it would be her duty to keep them from disturbing everyone. She began to plan various forms of entertainment calculated to keep them as quiet as possible.

'We're almost there,' said Mr Burns suddenly and turned the car off the road on to a narrow winding lane leading to the sea. Sure enough, she could see the coast now, high cliffs and sparkling water and here and there a red roofed white painted villa tucked away behind the trees growing thicker on either side of them. They drove past them all though and didn't stop until the sea was only a few hundred yards away down below, and they turned into a sandy drive leading to a handsome villa surrounded by a garden stuffed to choking point with flowers.

'We've been here before,' explained Mr Burns, 'there's a swimming pool round the back and steps down to the beach.' He stopped before the wide porch and got out. 'I'll carry these two in first—nice if they stay asleep for a bit longer. Can you manage Dee?'

She, following him inside, had Dee under one arm and wondered whose car it was parked beside the house and then forgot it while she admired the cool splendour of the hall; terra cotta tiles and white plastered walls and beautiful rugs and some rather uncomfortable looking chairs around the walls. She followed Mr Burns upstairs and discovered that there was a small dark woman ahead of them, leading the way. 'You'll be here,' Mr Burns told her and went in in front of her into a high-ceilinged room with closed shutters and a bed with an ornately carved head board; there were doors on either side, a bathroom and the children's room, shuttered against the heat. He lowered the still sleeping twins on to one of the beds and rubbed his arms. 'They are getting heavy,' he observed and glanced at Dee. 'She's due for a feed, isn't she? There's some made up in the car in the freezer bag, isn't there? I'll fetch it for you and ask Maria to send you up a tray of tea and something cold for the children when they wake. With luck you'll have time to shower and change before they rouse. Can you cope? Peggy will see to Mrs Beaufort and have a rest and we can have dinner when the children are in bed.'

Deborah said that of course she could manage, in her serene voice and added: 'If the children wake can we go into the garden? We'll stay in the shade and they can make more noise outside.'

'A good idea. Mrs Beaufort will rest I expect, but Peggy and I will be around in a couple of hours.'

Deborah inspected the room while she waited for her tea; it was pleasantly cool and dim and the furniture was of dark wood and very simple. There were a few rugs on the tiled floor and a gaily coloured bedspread. She approved of what she saw, just as she approved of the bathroom and the simply furnished room the children were in. She unpacked her overnight bag and called a quiet 'come in' when someone knocked on the door. It was Maria, unsmiling and polite, bearing a tray with a welcome teapot and a plate of little cakes and following hard on her heels, Mrs Burns.

'Nanny, can you manage for a bit? I'm putting Mother to bed and I'm going to lie down for an hour. This evening we'll work out some kind of time table between us.'

'Everything is fine, Mrs Burns. I expect Mrs Beaufort's pretty tired—let me know if I can help in any way. I expect we'll go outside once the twins wake. I'll get Dee fed and changed and take her with us in the carry-cot.'

Mrs Burns disappeared looking relieved and Deborah drank the teapot dry and then, with one eye on the twins, had a quick shower and changed into a cotton dress. Just in time, they woke together, demanded drinks and wanted to know where they were and what they were going to do. Deborah told them while she fed Deirdre, put them into cotton shirts and shorts, rubbed their small plump persons with lotion and suggested that they should creep downstairs and into the garden. It was cooler now and she opened the shutters and then, with Dee asleep in her carry-cot and the twins trotting behind her, went downstairs. She had slapped lotion on as much of her as she could reach and tied her hair back with a ribbon. They crossed the hall silently and went out through the open door. The first thing she saw was Professor Beaufort, leaning up against an orange tree, one arm flung round the thin shoulders of a girl of ten years or so.

She stood gaping at him, her gentle mouth a little open, while the twins made a concerted rush to wind their arms round his legs, their voices shrill with delight.

'Hush,' she whispered fiercely, 'don't disturb everyone.' He said 'Hullo Nanny. Not that you look in the least like one at the moment. Did we surprise you? Shock is perhaps the better word ... This is my daughter Eleanor, we arrived yesterday.'

Deborah smiled, said hullo and wondered why she suddenly felt depressed. Eleanor, giving her a rather shy smile, looked at her with her father's blue eyes. She was a pale child and later on she would be pretty with all that fair curly hair tumbling around her shoulders. She said in a voice as shy as her smile: 'Shall I show you the garden and the way down the steps to the beach?'

'Would you? Simon and Suzy can't wait to see everything,' Deborah grinned. 'Me too,' she added honestly. She supposed that Eleanor would join the nursery party and leave the professor and his wife free, and after all one more child didn't make all that difference and she was old enough to help with the twins if they became too boisterous.

The professor waved them a casual goodbye and went to the house and she found that her depression was strongly mingled with pleasure at seeing him again, which, considering she didn't like him in the very least, seemed strange. She wondered what his wife would be like and then pushed all thought of that to the back of her head so that she could give her attention to the children, capering along each side of Eleanor; they liked her, that was obvious. Deborah, with Dee awake for once and peering contentedly from her basket, followed them along a path bordered by a tangle of flowers and shrubs, which ended at a vast expanse of lawn and at one side a swimming pool. The twins instantly demanded to get into it and indeed Deborah eyed its cool blue water with longing, but she pointed out with cunning that she had nothing with her no towels, no swim suits . . .

'We don't need swim suits,' declared Simon.

'No, love but I do,' she pointed out reasonably, 'and you can't go in without me. Look, it's getting on for bedtime anyway. Shall we put everything ready for the morning and come here before breakfast?' She glanced at Eleanor and smiled, and the girl said: 'I'll come too, please, Nanny.'

'Of course. I'll ask Mummy if she will have Dee for half an hour.' She pretended not to see Simon's turned down mouth, and said briskly: 'Now what about that path down to the beach? Is it close by, Eleanor?'

The path was really a gentle zigzag of easy steps, ending on warm yellow sand; a small cove, sheltered by rocks on either side and no one else in sight. 'May we paddle?' asked Eleanor, 'I'll take care of the twins. It's quite safe here; Daddy and I went swimming this morning . . .'

Deborah perched on a handy rock by the water's edge, her hand on Dee's basket, and watched them with envy. The water was a clear, bright blue, she would have liked to have torn off her clothes and swum for hours. Perhaps, when they had settled in,

Mrs Burns would tell her when she could be free, so that she could spend her leisure here, swimming and lolling around; wearing a sunhat, of course, and even that wouldn't stop the freckles. Not that anyone was likely to notice them.

They all wandered back presently, the twins quite content after their paddle, Dee asleep again and Eleanor, now that she had got over her shyness, full of plans for picnics and outings and a trip along the coast in one of the fishermen's boats. Deborah, listening with only half an ear, knowing her role from previous experience. Dee was too small to take on such trips; she remembered the countless times she had been left at home with a baby or a toddler while everyone else made off joyfully, intent on a day out. After all, she reminded herself, it was her job, that was what she was paid for.

They found the others on the patio, lounging in comfortable chairs, with a tray of iced drinks on the table between them. Mrs Burns beamed at them all: 'There you are my dears. Have they been good, Nanny? Now it's supper for you and then bed, we've had a long day.'

Deborah looked away from the tempting contents of the glass jugs on the table; she longed for a cool drink but if the children were to have their supper it was unlikely that she would get one.

'Nanny needs a drink,' observed the professor, and got up out of his lounger. 'I'm going to take the children to see the kittens in the garage while she has it.'

He collected the three of them, picked up Dee out of her basket and deposited her on her mother's lap, and waved Deborah to a seat, while Mr Burns got up and poured a drink for her. She sat down, feeling awkward, like a gatecrasher, and watched the professor wandering off with his party.

'He's marvellous with the children,' declared Mrs Burns, 'and Eleanor gets on so well with the twins—you won't mind if she tags along with you, Nanny?'

'Not in the least, Mrs Burns—she's a sweet little girl and the twins adore her don't they? What a heavenly place this is.'

'Mmm we've been coming here for years. Have you all you want in your room? Do say if you need anything else. There's Maria, who housekeeps for us and two girls who come in each day—they'll see to the rooms and the beds and the washing. Mother will have to take things easily for a bit, but we'll get into a routine in a day or two. Once the children are in bed and we've had dinner, we'll put our heads together and work something out.' She turned her head to watch her brother and the children coming through the garden and Deborah got up, picked up Dee from her mother's lap and stood waiting for them.

'Supper's in the dining room,' said Mrs Burns, 'and there's plenty of hot water for baths, you'll be all right with Dee? She can sit on your lap . . .'

The professor had handed over the children unfussily, now he took the baby from Deborah and tucked her under one arm. 'Dee hasn't spoken to me yet—she shall sit with me until the children have finished their supper.' And he sat down with the infant, leaving Deborah to shepherd her charges into the house, sit them at table in the richly dark oak and leather dining room, and serve them their suppers. Eleanor sat with them explaining that when she was on holiday with her father she usually had her supper with him, but if Deborah didn't mind, she'd have it now and help her with the twins. 'Then perhaps I can help you to unpack,' she suggested.

Deborah smiled at her; she was a nice child and perhaps not quite as happy as she should be, she was too quiet for a start. Deborah wondered about her mother and hoped that someone would tell her sooner or later where she was, or if she were alive. No one had mentioned her.

She was to know soon enough. Two hours later, with the twins fast asleep, Dee fed and tucked up and herself in an Indian cotton dress and wearing a little more make-up than usual, she went downstairs. Mrs Burns had said dinner at half-past eight and it wanted five minutes to that hour. In the hall she paused, not quite sure where to go; she couldn't hear voices, only the faint clash of pots and pans from the kitchen part of the house. Perhaps it would be better if she went back to her room and waited for a gong. She turned on her heel and the professor said from somewhere behind her: 'No, don't go back to your room. The others aren't down yet—come and have a drink.'

He led the way outside, offered her a chair and went to the tray of drinks set ready. 'Something long and cool?' he suggested. 'I do hope Eleanor hasn't been a nuisance . . .'

'Of course not,' Deborah heard her voice a bit too loud and indignant, 'she's such a nice child and a great help with the twins. When they were in bed she helped me unpack. She's in bed herself now, reading.'

'Yes, I know, I've been up to see her.' He gave her a long considered glance over his glass. 'I'm glad that you get on well together. You have been wondering about her mother?'

'Yes,' said Deborah baldly.

'She died six years ago; she left us a year previously.

Eleanor doesn't remember her. She has a governess; a nice old fashioned maiden lady who conceals a clever brain under a mild exterior, her name is Miss Timmis.'

'She's not here?'

'No, she's having a well earned holiday. Which is what we are all having with the exception of yourself Deborah.'

She overlooked the Deborah and said a little tartly: 'I take my holidays between jobs, Professor Beaufort.'

'You must have the constitution of an ox and the temper of an angel.'

She looked away from him. 'What a curious mixture you must find me, professor, a gorgon with a mouth like a rat trap, and ox—a strong ox—with an angelic temper.'

He said blandly: 'You forget the sandy hair and the green eyes, they all add up to something quite out of the ordinary.'

She looked at him then and found him smiling. 'They add up to a children's nurse,' she told him soberly.

They dined presently in a leisurely fashion on melon soaked in port wine, *lulas recheadas* (which after she had eaten it Deborah discovered was squid embellished with egg yolk and tomatoes), ham and onion, a salad and *pudim fla* which she had no difficulty in recognising as egg custard. There was little time to talk before it was time to give Dee her feed; over coffee Mrs Burns suggested a flexible routine to be gone into thoroughly later on. 'Meals all together,' she suggested, 'but the children will wake early, Nanny, perhaps you could let them play in the garden—the nursery's overlooking the lawn isn't it? You could keep an eye on them while you see to Dee?'

Deborah had reservations about that, the twins needed two eyes on them all the time, that was something she would have to work out for herself. She murmured politely and Mrs Burns went on: 'Breakfast at half-past eight; Mother will have hers in her room, then we can all do our own thing until lunch time. Lunch at half-past twelve and the children must rest for a couple of hours unless we're picnicking, of course. You must have some free time—perhaps after tea for an hour or two? If the children have their supper at half-past six, that would give you time to go for a swim or write those letters or something. I daresay we shall go out quite a lot once we're rested— we won't always be able to take Dee—you won't mind being here with her? Maria will look after you, of course.' Mrs Burns smiled suddenly: 'It'll give you a break from the twins—isn't it a blessing that Dee's such a placid child?'

Deborah smiled and agreed, 'But if I don't give her a feed, she won't be placid at all,' she observed, and made a quiet exit, rather surprised when the professor got up and opened the door for her. Without saying anything though.

Dee was an easy baby; Deborah popped her back into her cot, undressed and showered, wrote a brief letter to her mother, took a final look at the twins and Eleanor in the little room across the passage, and then got into bed. A busy day, she reflected, and probably all the other days to come would be just as busy. It had been thoughtful of the professor to take the children off her hands for a few minutes; she still didn't like him of course, but perhaps she didn't dislike him quite as much, and she was sorry for him, poor man, with no wife and a child to bring up. She wondered about his wife and why she had left him and Eleanor—

perhaps he was a tyrant in his own home . . . she slept
on the thought.

She awoke to warm sunshine and the sound of a
nearby church bell chiming six o'clock. The twins
were still asleep but Dee was waking. Deborah fed
her, changed her and put her back in her cot and got
dressed herself. A swim in the pool would be heaven—
but quite impossible. She tied her hair back, slipped
bare feet into sandals and found the twins awake and
demanding to go out at once. They had the same idea
that she had: to get into the pool and she had to
explain why they couldn't, but no amount of
explaining helped! She wrestled them into shorts and
cotton tops and was brushing two tousled heads when
the door was opened and Eleanor put her head round.
'I heard you,' she said. 'May I come with you?'

Deborah beamed at her, 'Of course. The twins want
to go in the pool but they'll have to wait until after
breakfast, I can't leave Dee . . .'

The door behind Eleanor was pushed wide and the
professor, looking huge in a towelling robe, flung an
arm round his daughter. He wished them good
morning, dared them to utter a squeak and suggested—
in a voice which commanded more than suggested—
that there was no reason why they shouldn't all go to
the pool. The twins opened their mouths to shout
delightedly, 'Quiet!' He told them firmly then went
on: 'Eleanor, help them into their swim suits or
whatever they wear; Deborah, go and put on your
bikini and put Dee in her basket, we'll take it in turns
to mind her. Now look sharp everyone.'

Deborah found herself doing exactly as she had
been bidden; it took only a couple of minutes to get
out of her few garments and in to the newest of the
bikinis she had brought with her. She snatched up

Dee's basket, popped her in and went into the children's room. 'Towels?' she asked.

'In the changing room at the pool.' He looked at her briefly: 'Don't ever expect me to call you Nanny again,' he observed silkily. 'Shall we go?'

It was already warm and the garden smelled delicious. They ran over the lawn, the professor with a twin on each hand, Deborah with Dee and Eleanor skipping between them, all of them in silence. 'If anyone wakes up and hears us they might get cross, so mum's the word, especially you Simon.' The professor turned to grin at Deborah before he slid into the pool, helped the children in and began swimming up and down its length with first one then the other of them. Eleanor, Deborah noticed, could swim well, and between them she and her father ferried the little ones to and from each side with a lot of suppressed laughter and splashing.

'Now it's your turn,' the professor had heaved himself out and was sitting beside her, 'In you go, do you swim?'

She gave him a cold look. 'All Nannys swim,' she told him and slid in at the deep end to shoot down the pool to where Eleanor was playing with the twins. The water was warm; this would be where she would spend her precious free time, she decided as she joined the others in a watery game of ring o'roses.

The professor sat like Buddha with Dee cradled on his crossed legs. He watched the twins with tolerant amusement, his daughter with tender affection and then turned his gaze on to Deborah, bounding around like a twelve-year-old. He watched her for so long and so intently that a casual observer might have been forgiven for scenting a romance, but there was no romance in his face only a kind of intense speculation.

They all scrambled out presently and went in to dress for breakfast, leaving him there by the pool. It was half an hour before they met again at table, the twins in shorts and cotton tops and Eleanor and Deborah in sun dresses.

'A heavenly morning,' declared Mrs Burns from behind the coffee pot, 'who's for the beach?'

It seemed that they all were, although Mrs Burns stayed behind for a little while to settle Mrs Beaufort in a shady corner of the garden. Half way through the morning, when everybody was tired from being in the water and the twins had turned their energies to making sand castles, Deborah was asked—very nicely—if she would go back to the house and make sure that the old lady was all right. 'And don't bother to come down again,' said Mrs Burns, 'we'll be up for lunch in less than an hour, so I'll look after the children.'

Her husband and brother exchanged amused glances; Peggy was a good mother and a loving one but she had long ago devised a system of delegating maternal authority to whoever happened to be handy. She smiled at them both: 'I'm quite exhausted with all this heat, will you two keep an eye on them while I snatch a few minutes' peace?' She added generously: 'You can leave Dee here in her basket.'

Easily done since Dee was asleep. 'You're a humbug,' declared the professor equably, 'I pity Bill from the bottom of my heart.'

'Wait until you marry,' said Peggy. 'No don't answer that, I'm asleep.'

Eleanor had listened. 'If you ever marry again, Daddy, can it be someone just like Deborah, I do like her.'

'You mean, Nanny, darling?' asked Mrs Burns.

'She said I could call her Deborah: I'm too old to say nanny.'

'So you are love.' The professor had got to his feet. 'You and I are going for a short walk—we haven't had a talk for a long time have we?'

Eleanor took his hand. When they were well away from the others she asked: 'What about, Daddy?'

He flung an arm round her small shoulders. 'I've had a rather nice idea,' he began and started to explain it to her.

Back in the garden, Deborah fetched another jug of lemonade for Mrs Beaufort, walked her gently up and down in the shade for a short time, and then sat down on the grass at her feet. The sun was really warm now and despite the sun hat and sitting in the shade, her freckles were making a splendid show. They made her look very young and Mrs Beaufort said suddenly: 'You're nothing more than a child . . .'

'I'm twenty-three, Mrs Beaufort, and I've been trained for more than three years now.'

'Indeed? And no boy-friends?'

'No, I've lots of friends though. I think perhaps I'm not the kind of girl a man wants to marry.' She turned her head, her ordinary face lighted by a smile. 'Isn't it lucky that I like my job. After Christmas I shall look for a permanent post—you know, with some county family with hordes of children, so that I can stay with them forever.'

'You'd like that?'

'It's the next best thing to being married and having children of my own, isn't it?'

'I daresay it is. Peggy has been very lucky in her marriage; her husband adores her and the children are charming, which is a fortunate thing for I am sure she would have made a deplorable mess of a job and being single. As for Gideon—well, at least he has Eleanor—his wife left him when Eleanor was three years old. An American millionaire I think he was, it's a terrible thing to confess, but I was glad when she died in an accident a year later. There was no love left between them but it has changed him.' She gave a little chuckle: 'He's not quite a misogynist but he has cultivated an amused tolerance toward women. Some girl will come along one day and crack it wide open, and the sooner the better.'

They had lunch out of doors under the orange trees before Deborah took a sleepy pair of children up to their beds and set about feeding Dee. There were small chores to do after that, and she was hot and tired by the time they were done. She got on to her own bed and dozed until Simon came pattering in, asking for a drink, and while he had it she told him a story.

They went to the beach again before tea but this time Deborah didn't go into the water; Mrs Burns hadn't joined them and she sat with Dee while Mr Burns splashed around with the twins. They trooped up to the house presently and found the others sitting in the garden round a table laden with a teapot and plates of sandwiches and cake. It was the professor who observed presently: 'Isn't it about time Nanny had an hour to herself. It's cool enough now to play ball with the children.'

'I'll come with you,' said Eleanor eagerly as Deborah got up and before her father could say anything Deborah said cheerfully: 'Yes, do—we'll go for another swim shall we?' Although she longed to be alone just for an hour. All the same Eleanor was good company, they swam for a while and then strolled along the beach, letting the warm water wash round their feet, until Deborah glanced at her watch. 'Time to feed Dee,' she cried, 'my goodness I almost forgot.' She took the hand Eleanor held out. 'It's been fun, hasn't it?'

The twins didn't want to have their supper, neither did they want to go to bed, it took all Deborah's powers of persuasion to settle them for the night and by the time she had tidied the room and put out clean clothes for the morning, she had to rush through a shower and change of clothes, not wasting much time over her hair or her face. The freckles looked worse than ever, she decided, dabbing on powder and then washing it off again because they weren't to be disguised. She got downstairs with a couple of minutes to spare, and accepted the glass Mr Burns offered her.

'A lovely day,' observed Mrs Burns happily. 'I say, Nanny, you have caught the sun—have you something to put on your face? Those freckles . . .'

Everyone looked at her as she said quietly: 'Aren't they awful? I get them every summer and it makes no difference what I put on them.' It vexed her very much that she blushed as she spoke and that made the wretched things even more noticeable.

The professor started to talk about something else, turning attention away from her and she was grateful for that. He could be kind, she had discovered. After dinner, making the excuse that she was tired so that she wouldn't be the odd man out in the family, he had gone to the door with her. 'I hope Eleanor didn't spoil your free time,' he said quietly, 'that wasn't intended.' Then he added: 'We must make amends.'

CHAPTER FOUR

THERE was no sign of the professor making amends during the next few days, not that Deborah was at all sure what he had meant. Amends for what? Did he think that she expected to be free for hours on end? Or that she had minded having Eleanor for company when she was free? She dismissed the subject as being too trivial to think about, in any case she hadn't all that much time to sit about thinking. The days fell quickly into a pleasant pattern, if a hard working one, for the children were here there and everywhere; eating their meals out of doors, up at first light and never wanting to go to bed. Nonetheless, Deborah heard without rancour Mrs Burns' suggestion that they should drive along the coast to Cape St Vincent and have lunch out: 'That nice place at Sagres . . .'

'*Pousade do infante,*' murmured the professor.

Mrs Burns nodded. 'That's the one. Nanny you won't mind staying here with Dee, will you?' She smiled charmingly, 'you'll be glad of a nice quiet day with her. Maria will look after you and we'll be back in good time for the children to go to bed.'

Deborah agreed with ready cheefulness, forbearing to mention that Dee was cutting a tooth and had had a restless night so would probably have a restless day too. Perhaps it was just as well that everyone was going out so that she could give her her whole attention. At least for the moment the infant was sleeping which gave Deborah the chance to get the twins ready for their outing.

'I wish you were coming too,' said Eleanor softly as the party assembled at the front of the house. 'There's heaps of room because Daddy's taking his car and there is only me with him.'

'Another time, love,' promised Deborah and went to settle Mrs Beaufort in the front seat of the Burns' car, and then arranged the twins one each side of their mother in the back. 'We shall be very hot,' said Mrs Burns worriedly, and then: 'You're sure you'll be all right, Nanny?'

'Quite sure. Have a lovely day.' Deborah dropped a kiss on each twin's cheek, 'Bring me back some seaweed.'

Mr Burns drove off and she turned to the professor's car. 'Have a nice day,' she repeated and was engulfed in Eleanor's hug.

The professor was leaning against the bonnet: 'I heard Dee grizzling dreadfully during the night. Teething?'

He didn't look the kind of man to bother about childish ailments. Deborah said shortly: 'That's right, yes,' and then, 'I hope you have a lovely day.'

'You said that just now. When do you have your day off?'

She flushed slowly, 'Mrs Burns hasn't had time to discuss it with me,' she told him shortly. 'In any case . . .'

'It's none of my business,' he finished for her smoothly. 'Jump in, Eleanor and let us sample the delights of Cape St Vincent and Sagres.'

He drove off with a careless wave of the hand and Deborah waved back, not to him but to Eleanor, standing watching the little Fiat until it had reached the lane and disappeared. It was still early and the day stretched before her; she went indoors and changed into a bikini and put the sun hat and sun glasses on and carried the still sleeping Dee out into the garden setting her basket against one of the orange trees. It was pleasantly cool and shady and she sat, doing nothing until Dee woke and began to cry. Deborah took her out of the basket and sat her on her lap giving her a teething ring, but she went on wailing. It was too early for her feed so Deborah tucked her under her arm and wandered round the garden with her until presently the sobbing stopped. Fed and changed and for the moment content, Dee slept again and Deborah lay back, idly day-dreaming. To be married to a man who could provide luxurious villas for holidays and charter planes to get one there would be quite something. She wasn't envious of Mrs Burns, she was too sensible for that, but there was no harm in letting her imagination run riot for a bit. She wouldn't want a husband like Mr Burns though; he was a dear, kind and thoughtful and good natured and he spoilt Mrs Burns outrageously. Deborah thought that a man like him would get on her nerves after a time, but neither would she want to be bullied. The professor came near to doing that from time to time, perhaps not bullying, but certainly overriding anyone who didn't fall in with his suggestions. She was aware that she wasn't being quite fair but she busied herself thinking up all his faults and failings so that she could prove to herself that she was right.

The day wore on slowly with Dee getting more fractious as it became warmer, Deborah was walking up and down in the shade with her over one shoulder, longing for the tea which she saw no chance of getting, when the Fiat raced up the drive and stopped by the house. Eleanor and her father reached her at the same time. The professor stretched out an arm, transferred

Dee to his own shoulder and patted the small back with a large hand.

'Take Deborah into the house and see that she gets some tea,' he told Eleanor. His eye lighted on Deborah's face which was all ready to refuse. 'And you do as I say Debby.' His eyes skimmed the bikini. 'Since you're dressed for a swim, I suggest that you have one as soon as you've had tea.'

He marched off with Dee, and Eleanor tugged at Deborah's hand. 'Come on, Daddy's awfully good with babies and children—he frightens grown ups sometimes, but that's all.'

Quite enough too, thought Deborah, allowing herself to be led indoors to fall gratefully upon a plate of sandwiches and drain the teapot.

'Did you have a nice day?' She offered a sandwich to her companion.

'Lovely. We went to Prince Henry's Fort and watched the fishermen and went swimming at Sagres. Has Dee been crying all day?'

'Well, on and off, yes. The tooth's nearly through though. I daresay she'll be happier tomorrow, the poor poppet.'

'Aren't you tired, Deborah?'

She swallowed the rest of her tea and got up. 'Only a very little bit—that tea was lovely, I was beginning to think that I wouldn't get any.'

'Daddy drove back very fast because he said perhaps you'd need a break. Wasn't it lucky that we got home early?'

'Very, and I'm most grateful. Now I'm going back to Dee . . .'

'You haven't had your swim, Daddy said you had to have a swim.' Eleanor took her hand as they went back into the garden. 'There's heaps of time, the others hadn't even started when we left.'

There was no sign of the professor and Dee. Deborah stood uncertainly for a moment, and then, urged on by Eleanor, followed her down the path to the beach. The water was warm; she swam lazily, keeping an eye on Eleanor and left the sea reluctantly. They went back into the house and ten minutes later were back in the garden, both rather damp about the head but cool in sundresses.

The professor was lying under the trees, his niece spread over his chest asleep. He opened an eye as they reached him. 'The tooth's through, thank God. How nice and clean and cool you look.'

'The water was heaven and so was the tea. Thank you very much, Professor.'

'The pleasure was mine. I do hope that my sister hasn't any plans for this evening, I'm for early bed.' He glanced at his watch. 'They'll be here shortly. The twins have had a busy day I can tell you, with luck they'll gobble their supper and fall into bed.'

'They said they never wanted to go home again,' said Eleanor.

'Then we must remind them that the puppy will be waiting for them. Here they are now. I'll stay with Dee while you deal with the twins, Deborah.'

She collected them without loss of time, pausing only long enough to murmur sympathetically at Mrs Burns' rather plaintive remark that she was exhausted. Mrs Beaufort looked exhausted too, but the quicker the twins were fed and put to bed the sooner everyone could relax. For once they were angelic; eating their suppers with no fuss at all, submitting to lightning showers and pyjamas with the minimum of complaints, indeed they chattered happily about their day, only stopping when Deborah popped them into their beds and tucked them up. She went along to her own room then, made sure that she was presentable and then went downstairs. Mrs Burns was lying on one of the sofas in the sitting room. 'Bill's gone to see to something in the car and Dee's still asleep with Gideon; Eleanor's with them. I'm very weary, Nanny, will you be an angel and help Mother to bed? I think she should rest at once and have her dinner there, don't you?'

Mrs Burns was undoubtedly tired, Deborah told herself going back upstairs and tapping on Mrs Beaufort's door. She was tired herself, but she forgot that when she saw Mrs Beaufort sitting in a chair by the window.

'I've had such a lovely day,' she told Deborah, 'but you know, I'm too tired to get undressed! Isn't that silly?'

'It was a long day,' observed Deborah, 'and of course you're tired. Mrs Burns asked me to give you a hand and I'll tell Maria to bring you up a tray and you can have it sitting up in bed. That way you can go to sleep just whenever you feel like it. Now let's get you to bed . . .'

It took quite a while; Mrs Beaufort wasn't to be hurried and she wanted to talk about her day, so it was well past the time for Dee's feed by the time Deborah had been to the kitchen to arrange for Mrs Beaufort's supper and Dee still had to be got ready for bed. Of course, Mrs Burns might have started . . .

She hadn't. The professor came in from the garden with Dee draped tearfully over one shoulder just as Deborah came into the room.

'Aren't you a bit late, Nanny?' asked Mrs Burns pleasantly. 'Did you get Mother into bed and see to her supper?'

The professor spoke before she could. 'Do I understand that Deborah has fed the twins, put them to bed, put Mother to bed too and now has to feed Dee and get her into bed as well? Isn't that a bit much, even for a highly trained nanny, my dear?'

'But you're so capable, aren't you, Nanny? And you've had all day without any of us . . .'

The professor shook his head at her. 'Deborah's been up half the night with Dee—she's cut a tooth, and I'll wager she's had a long hard day of it.'

Deborah stood between them, feeling a fool. She snapped: 'I'm perfectly all right, Professor.' And whisked Dee away from him and out of the room, leaving him laughing softly and Mrs Burns bewildered. 'She's a girl in a thousand,' she observed, 'but it is her job and I pay her well.'

The professor stopped laughing. 'And make the fullest use of her, just as you do of Bill and me and anyone else who happens to be around. Look, love, let her have the day off tomorrow—heaven knows she's earned it. I've got to go back to Lagos, I'll be happy to give her a lift there and back.'

Mrs Burns gave him a quick look. 'What a splendid idea—do you suppose Eleanor would stay here with us? She's so marvellous with the twins—we could go on the beach . . .'

'I'm sure she'll be delighted.' She watched him stroll away, out into the garden. Mrs Burns broached the subject of a day off during dinner: 'And as Gideon has to go into Lagos tomorrow he can give you a lift.'

Deborah opened her mouth to refuse and then closed it again when she saw the faint, knowing smile on the professor's lips. 'Thank you,' she agreed sedately, 'that would be very convenient, I should like

to explore the town and do some shopping—presents
you know.'

'Embroidery and pottery,' said Mrs Burns rather
vaguely, 'the shops shut in the afternoon, but I
daresay you'll find something to do . . .'

She smiled kindly at Deborah; she was a dear girl
and so good with the children, and she had quite
forgotten that until Gideon had mentioned it she had
overlooked the fact that Deborah, with the exception
of the brief hour or so after tea, had had no time to
herself. She added: 'You go and enjoy yourself Nanny,
I'll be able to manage—Bill's here to help and
Eleanor . . .'

They left directly after breakfast while it was still
cool. Deborah wore a sundress with a little jacket and
had her swim suit packed in the roomy straw bag Mrs
Burns had lent her. She had rammed her sun hat on
top of her piled up hair and put on her sun glasses,
then spent a few moments regretfully examining her
freckles which seemed worse than ever. The rest of
her was nicely tanned, as the professor pointed out to
her as they drove off. 'I like the freckles too,' he added
with casual friendliness. He talked easily as they
drove, pointing out various things which might
interest her but never once mentioning the children or
her work so that after a while Deborah began to feel
that she too was on holiday without a care in the
world—no teething baby, no rumbustious twins; she
sniffed the warm air and relaxed.

The professor slowed down as they reached the
town, pointing out the fish market, the fort and the
bus station on the boulevard by the river. When he
stopped at a car park Deborah asked: 'Shall I meet you
here when you are going back, or shall I catch a bus?'

'Let's talk about that over coffee,' he invited, 'but

first we'll go to the bank, if you don't mind—they
close at noon and only open for a couple of hours in
the afternoon.'

The town was still fairly full with tourists and the
narrow streets were crowded. Once the business at the
bank was attended to he then turned up a narrow lane
and ushered her into a shop selling pottery and
embroidery, but he didn't stop there going on, down a
passage into a coffee shop.

Over their coffee she said again: 'If you'd tell me
what bus to catch?'

He leaned back in the narrow cane chair which
creaked abominably.

'Oh, I'm having a day off too, I was hoping we might
do some sightseeing and I've some things to buy—I
could do with your advice.' He watched her face. 'If you
don't care for the idea, don't mind saying so.'

She stared at him across the small table. 'Won't I
bore you?'

'No.' He beckoned the waiter for more coffee. 'Shall
we do the shopping first and put it in the car? We can
lunch at one of the local restaurants, they are very
simple but the food is usually good. Everything shuts
until four o'clock so we could drive to Rocha, it's not
far, and have a swim.'

'That sounds heavenly if you are sure?'

'I'm sure. Finished? You'd better use the loo here,
some of them are a bit primitive, but Eleanor's given
this one the okay.'

Deborah went meekly and presently found him in
the pottery shop. 'The trouble is,' he observed, 'these
things tend to break on the way home. I want
something for my housekeepr. What do you suggest?'

Deborah started to poke round the embroidery. 'Is
she house proud?' she wanted to know.

'Oh God, yes.'

'This then,' decided Deborah, picking out an exquisitely embroidered teacloth. 'Aren't they gorgeous? I think I'll have one for Mother.'

They wandered out to the street, stopping to look in shop windows while the professor patiently worked out the prices into pounds and pence. After an hour, laden now with odds and ends which had caught her fancy, they sat down in the tiny square in the centre of the town to drink orange juice before strolling back to the car. Empty handed once more, they went back into the town and went into a small rather bare restaurant in one of the main streets.

'You've been here before, of course,' said Deborah. 'I expect you know all the restaurants and cafés.'

'Most of them. This one's plain but the food's good and the fish is excellent. What about grilled sea bream and a salad? And Vinho Verde to go with it?'

They sat idly, not talking much but at ease with each other, drinking their wine and watching their lunch being cooked at the back of the restaurant.

'You may find dessert rather sweet—I should have an ice,' counselled the professor. 'I shall have *cabeiro*—that's goat's milk cheese.'

It was hot when they went into the street again and got into the car to drive the short distance to Rocha.

'Just look at that beach!' exclaimed Deborah as they drove slowly along the boulevard. It wasn't very wide nor very long, but there were shops facing the sea, smart boutiques and coffee shops and newspaper kiosks.

The professor turned the car into the car park behind a large hotel built on the very edge of the beach then took Deborah's hand and led her inside.

'Sit there while I have a word,' he said and went

over to the desk. He came back very shortly with two keys. 'There are changing rooms at the bottom of the steps leading to the beach. Here's your key—let the desk have it before we go on to the beach, now stay here while I fetch our things.'

The beach wasn't crowded just nicely filled and the water was warm and very clear. Deborah, free from keeping an eye on the children, swam happily out to sea only vaguely aware that the professor was beside her. Presently she turned on to her back and found him idling close by.

'It must be very hot in the summer,' she observed, her eyes closed.

'Very—this is the best time of the year—and spring, of course, but it's not quite as warm.' He rolled over. 'Race you back?'

He allowed her to win and they lay on the sand under a canvas awning, presently Deborah went to sleep. When she woke up the professor was sitting beside her, watching her. She wondered why he looked so intent, as though he was trying to decide something and then forgot all about it when he suggested that they should have another swim before tea.

They sat on the verandah and drank a surprisingly English tea, and ate little, very sweet cakes, then walked along the wide sand in the late afternoon cool.

'Oughtn't I to be going back?' asked Deborah.

'Only if you would like to, you're not expected. I said we'd be back around midnight.'

'Midnight?' She turned surprised green eyes on his bland face.

'They dine late here you know. We could go back now and sit over a drink.'

She stood still facing him. 'You spent the whole day

taking me around. I'm most grateful but there was no need—I'm quite used to getting along on my own, and I expect you've done all this before.'

'I'm not going to make the obvious answer to that. Just reflect that I could have left you at the car park this morning.' He took her arm. 'I need a drink.'

Sitting outside a wine bar on the boulevard he asked suddenly 'What do you think of Eleanor?'

'Nice,' said Deborah promptly. 'Shy at first but so—so loving if you know what I mean. Is she like her mother?'

She wished she hadn't said that. The professor's face froze into an inscrutable mask. 'No.' She hoped that he would say something else, but he didn't so she went on hurriedly: 'Oh, well anyway—she's a darling. The twins adore her and she's good company—rather grown up for ten years old.'

'That is probably because she has no mother; Miss Timmis is elderly—more like a kindly aunt, my housekeeper is no longer in her first youth either, and nor for that matter am I. Which is perhaps the reason why Eleanor is less of a child than she should be.'

'But she is quite happy?'

'She could be happier—it's rather on my conscience. That's why we came here with Peggy and Bill and the children—they're a family.'

He sounded bitter and she wanted to say something sympathetic, but she had no chance for he went on in his usual casual way: 'Let's stroll back to the hotel and have dinner.'

The meal was excellent and very leisurely, so it was well after ten o'clock by the time they got back into the car. The evening had darkened and the sea glittered under a full moon. A night for romance, thought Deborah sleepily and wished, just for a

moment, that she was sitting beside some young man
who was hopelessly in love with her, with the promise
of a delightful future and undying devotion before her
. . . She gasped when the professor said silkily: 'The
night's wasted on us, isn't it? It's a night for lovers;
not a not-so-young widower and a dedicated nanny!'

'I am not dedicated!' declared Deborah quickly, her
voice tart.

'There's hope for me yet,' said the professor, the
silk back in his voice.

'Don't spoil my lovely day making silly jokes.'

He shot the car up the drive and stopped silently
before the villa. Before he got out he said gently: 'I'm
sorry, Debby. It was a lovely day—I've enjoyed every
minute of it, thank you for your company.'

She got out and stood beside him. 'I enjoyed it too,
thank you for taking me.' She smiled up at him and he
swept her close and kissed her gently but thoroughly
too. She stared at him in utter surprise before she ran
indoors.

The twins, refreshed by a sound night's sleep,
welcomed her enthusiastically when she got up to feed
Dee at six o'clock. They climbed into her bed and sat
telling her in a chorus of yesterday's pleasure. She
responded suitably, saw to Dee's comfort then washed
and dressed before going into the garden.

Eleanor usually joined them at their early morning
games, but there was no sign of her and it wasn't until
they were all sitting at breakfast that Mrs Burns
remarked casually that Eleanor and her father had
gone off at five o'clock, long before anyone else was
stirring, to go fishing. 'Gideon persuaded one of the
local fishermen to let them go with him—they drove
into Lagos and planned to go on board there—they
won't be back until this evening. Nanny, we're going

into Portimao before lunch, I must get my hair done. If we're not back before twelve go ahead and have yours and settle the children for their rest, will you?'

Deborah hadn't really expected the Burns and Mrs Beaufort back for lunch and she was quite right, she coaxed the twins into their beds, saw to Dee and went to sit in the garden. It was hot and airless, and although the sky was blue she had the nasty feeling that there would be a storm before long. The sunlight became more and more brassy and the birds stopped singing. She watched the skies darken and pretended not to mind when she heard the first rumble of thunder. She made herself stay where she was until the next rumble, but then her calm deserted her and she scampered for the house. There was no one about; the two girls who came to help every day had long since gone home and Maria went to her own little house down the lane each afternoon and wouldn't be back until it was time to prepare the evening meal. Deborah peered into the kitchen just to make sure that she had gone; the tea tray was ready on the table but there was no sign of Maria, she hadn't expected to find her anyway. She went upstairs, flinching at a flash of lightning, and found the children still sound asleep. It would have been nice if they woke up, she thought wistfully, the house seemed very silent and getting darker every minute. She went back downstairs and then tore back up again as there was a vivid flash of lightning and the children woke, screaming with fright, rivalling the thunder and waking Dee.

Deborah picked up Dee, popped Suzy on to Simon's bed and sat down on its edge. It was far too warm with the twins wrapped round her as close as they could get and the baby on her lap, but just for the moment it was impossible to budge them; they bellowed at each flash and she could hardly blame them—she would have liked to bellow herself.

It started to rain, bucketing down, crashing on to the roof, overflowing the gutters, adding to the noise. Deborah gave up trying to speak, for there was no way of making herself heard. The storm was right overhead now, crashing and banging round the house with hardly a pause. She hoped that Mr and Mrs Burns were still in Portimao or had at least taken shelter. Only a madman would drive through in such weather. She hadn't allowed herself to think about the professor and Eleanor; out at sea the storm would surely be quite terrifying. She worried about it for a few minutes and found that she was worrying just as much about the professor as his daughter, which would never do. She mustn't allow a pleasant day with him to change her opinion of him; he could turn on the charm, she knew that now, but he could be just as beastly if he felt like it.

Somewhere close-by a tree crashed down and Suzy screamed, burying her head against Deborah and at the same time she saw the car lights coming up the drive. The Burns, she thought thankfully and then: supposing it wasn't? Supposing it was someone wanting shelter? Or just someone? She swallowed her fright and listened in vain for sounds other than the storm. The front door bell, and oh lord, she had left the door open when she came in. Surely the Burns would call out as they came into the house? And it couldn't be the professor and Eleanor because they were being tossed around somewhere at sea.

She had left the door open when she had come into the children's room and in the brief pause between the thunder and the lightning she heard steps on the stairs.

She was so frightened that she could hardly breathe; the storm didn't matter any more, only the steps drowned now in celestial noise. She had gone very white, clutching the children close to her, not knowing what to do.

When the professor loomed in the doorway, his clothes plastered to him, water forming pools round his feet, she could only stare speechlessly.

His hullo was laconic, although his sharp glance had taken in Deborah's ashy face. He squelched across the floor, picked up the twins and said: 'Let's go down to the kitchen, shall we?' And he waited while she got to her feet with Dee under her arm before shooing her gently downstairs.

Eleanor was in the kitchen, taking off her wringing wet clothes. She grinned at Deborah over her shoulder and said in an excited voice: 'Isn't this simply super? You should have been there, Deborah, you'd have loved it!'

Deborah smiled with a shaking mouth and felt the professor's large wet hand on her shoulder, pressing her gently into a chair. 'I frightened you—very thoughtless of me, I'm sorry. Sit there and we'll all have a cup of tea. But first of all I'd better get out of these wet things. I'll take the twins with me, and Eleanor can stay here with you. There's a towel she can wrap herself in; I'll bring down her dressing gown.'

He loomed over Deborah and for once his face was full of concern and kindness, but she hardly noticed; she was busy enough struggling to regain her usual calm. She was almost back to normal, despite several violent thunder claps and the vivid lightning, when he returned clad in slacks and a shirt, carrying Eleanor's dressing gown and trailed by the twins.

The electricity had been cut off soon after the storm began but he went through the cupboards until he found an old primus stove and lit it, filled a kettle and got out the tea pot. And all the while he kept up a rumbling monologue about nothing much, making the children laugh while Deborah sat as stiff as a board with fright, clutching Dee and hardly speaking, furious with herself for allowing her feelings to show but quite unable to do anything about it. She avoided the professor's eye, drank her tea and almost dropped the mug when another tree came crashing down close to the house. The professor sat opposite her at the table, a twin on each knee with Eleanor close to him; she found herself wishing that she could be close to him too, he gave the impression, probably erroneous, that while he was there nothing awful was going to happen. She watched his face, wondering what he had to laugh about when she was straining every nerve not to burst into tears along with the children, but she didn't look away quickly enough and he caught her eye. The smile he gave her was kind, but just sufficiently mocking to make her sit up and lift her chin. She remembered that he had called her a gorgon; the memory helped enormously and she felt her courage creeping back, after all the storm couldn't last much longer. She flinched as the room was filled by vivid blue lightning and the thunder tumbled and crashed around the house. In the quiet pause before the next deafening din he observed: 'I think the storm is moving away.' And he was right; surprisingly fifteen minutes later the sun was shining from a blue sky and the ground was steaming. The children, their fright forgotten, demanded to go down to the beach. 'And why not?' asked their uncle. 'That is if Nanny permits it?'

What a stuffy creature he must think her. Deborah said quietly: 'I think it's a marvellous idea. I'll get Dee's basket and the swim suits.' She paused: 'If you wouldn't mind keeping an eye on the twins for a minute?'

He reached out and took Dee from her. 'Eleanor's got to put on something—it's too late for the children to go into the water. I'm afraid you've missed your time off Deborah.'

'It doesn't matter. I'd have been petrified if I'd been on my own, anyway.' She looked up at him gravely. 'I'm a coward about storms, I'm sorry.'

He lifted an eyebrow. 'You don't have to apologise to me, my dear. We all have our Achilles' heel.'

He hardly spoke to her again, but ran races with the children at the water's edge while she sat with Dee. They were returning to the house when Mr and Mrs Burns and Mrs Beaufort returned and the next ten minutes were taken up with rather excited talk on the part of Mrs Burns, and very exaggerated accounts of bravery on behalf of the twins. Deborah led them away presently, gave them their supper, saw to the baby and put them to bed. She had been afraid that after all the afternoon's excitement they wouldn't take kindly to the idea of sleep, but they gave her no more than ten minutes of tantrums before falling asleep with welcome suddenness, leaving her free to go as quickly as she could to her room, at last free to change her dress and do things to her face and hair. It hadn't been much of a day she reflected, pinning her sandy tresses back rather severely, the storm had been bad enough, but having to admit to near panic in front of the professor was far worse. He must think her a spineless creature. Not that that mattered in the least; she couldn't care less what he thought of her, although she had to admit to a strong desire to do something which would take that tolerant, faintly mocking smile off his handsome face.

She went downstairs presently and found everyone on the patio sitting in the cool of the evening over their drinks. She accepted Mr Burns' offer of a long, cool drink without enquiring as to what he intended to put into it, and sat down in the chair Mrs Burns was patting.

'Such a dreadful afternoon,' said that lady, 'I've never been so terrified in all my life. I'm still shaking . . .'

Deborah took a look; her employer looked as cool and unruffled as a newly scooped ice cream, moreover she looked very pretty in a vividly patterned cotton dress that Deborah hadn't seen before.

'How lucky for you that you were here,' went on Peggy Burns. 'Nice and safe in the house and the children seemed to have behaved splendidly. Sorry about your free time though—we'll have to make it up to you . . .'

The professor, lolling back in a wide cane chair, spoke: 'I don't know about Deborah, but I thought I'd stroll along as far as the village after dinner; there's a café there where someone sings *fado*, perhaps she'll come with me.' He added dryly: 'The children are all tucked up and sleeping, so she can leave them with a clear conscience.'

'Splendid!' cried his sister not giving Deborah a chance to say a word. 'A lovely little outing for her and, as you say, the children won't disturb me—I really am too exhausted to cope with them until I've had a good night's sleep . . .'

No one, Deborah reflected, had asked her if she wished to go out with the professor. She felt like a hungry dog offered a bone, but unlike the dog, not over keen to take it. The matter was decided for her: 'We can walk along the beach path,' said Professor Beaufort, 'enjoy the *fado* and come back along the lane.' He yawned, 'Or the other way round. It doesn't really matter.'

This stung Deborah into speech. 'So kind of you to suggest it,' she said with slight waspishness, 'but I think I'm too tired . . .'

She was overruled; even Mr Burns, who seldom took part in any argument, was against her. She ate her dinner meekly while inwardly fuming.

It was a splendid night when they set out to walk along the beach path; a romantic night, with a full moon slowly turning everything to a silvery day, and the faintest of breezes stirring the warm air.

They discussed the storm at some length, with the professor going into rather boring details about weather and so on—deliberately she thought. Well, it made something to talk about anyway. But once they were sitting at a small table at the *casa de fado* everything was different. Deborah hadn't been sure what to expect, but the black clad *fadista* pouring out her melancholy song of regrets and sadness, absorbed her whole attention. She drank whatever the professor ordered, ate the bits and pieces he offered her from time to time and sat enraptured, her melancholy almost as deep as the singer's, but somehow more pleasurable.

The singer went away presently and the professor asked mildly: 'Enjoying it Debby?'

'Oh, yes, very much. I've never heard anything like it before, though I suppose you have. Is it a kind of folk song?'

'Yes, and very old. There are two kinds—the

traditional, which you hear in and around Lisbon and this one, the Coimbra *Fado*—I suppose you would call it regional.'

They stayed late, with Deborah unaware of the time and the professor watching her with a faint, amused smile. When at last she glanced at her watch he answered her horrified squeak of surprise with a reasonable: 'Well, there's no need to fuss—Peggy's quite able to feed Dee for once and I imagine that the twins won't stir until morning. You don't have to look so guilty, you spend long hours with the children and never complain.'

'But it's my job.'

'So you have reminded me on several occasions. Would you like to be free, Debby?'

She had had a little too much to drink and her tongue was running riot. 'Yes, oh, yes. To do what I want to do—have a huge garden and dogs and cats running in and out and buy lovely clothes just whenever I wanted to and travel.' She stopped suddenly 'That's just pipe dreaming—I expect everyone has those, but that's not real life, is it?'

He didn't say anything but got up when she did and walked beside her out of the café and into the village street, taking her arm, which, actually, she was glad of because the fresh air after the stuffiness of the café and all the wine she had drunk, was making her a little dizzy.

'We'll go back the way we came,' he said. 'It's much prettier and the moon is still up.'

They walked in silence for some time until Deborah, finding it awkward, said the first thing which came into her head: 'The moon makes it very romantic, doesn't it?'

'Indeed, yes. Are you romantic, Deborah?'

'Only sometimes, mostly I'm too busy ... My last reference said that I was a sensible, level-headed girl with a realistic attitude to life. That's not romantic, is it?' She sighed, 'And I daresay it's quite true too!'

Their stroll had come to a halt and he turned her round to face him.

'Will you marry me, Deborah?' asked the professor. And at her look of utter astonishment: 'Oh, there's no question of romance and love. I like you enormously, for your reference is correct, you know and over and above that you're kind and serene and quiet and Eleanor is very fond of you; in time I think that she could love you. She needs someone like you—Miss Timmis is all that a governess should be, but she's no longer young and she has never aspired to the maternal. She'll remain with us, of course, probably for the rest of her life in some capacity or another, but she will be the first to agree that Eleanor needs a mother—you are a little young perhaps, but all the same you have become very dear to her. I am away from home from time to time, but life won't be dull for you—you will have your garden and your dogs and cats—a couple of donkeys and a pony too, and I can promise you that you may buy all the clothes you want. The question is: what should I be depriving you of? Perhaps there is someone who wants to marry you?'

She shook her head silently.

'Or you might wish to wait for a more romantic proposal?'

She shook her head again. 'That's not very likely.'

'You would like children of your own, and not other people's?'

She looked away from him, to the smooth moonlit sea with the lights from the fishing boats reflected in the water. 'Yes, it would have to be a very special reason for me to—to accept. I'm sorry, it's very kind of you to ask me.' She added slowly: 'I didn't know you liked me even.'

'I've already said that I do.' His voice was pleasantly bland with no sign of what he really thought. 'Do you like me, Deborah?'

'It's a funny thing; I didn't at first—you called me a gorgon, you know and you laughed at me a lot, but then when we came here and I met Eleanor, I began to like you—yes, I suppose I like you now.'

'Well, that's something. All the same, you are refusing me?'

Deep down inside her she felt regret. 'Yes, you see I'd like to have a husband who loved me and whom I loved, otherwise I'd just as soon stay as I am.'

He turned her round and took her arm again. 'Well, at least you're honest. I'm sorry, Debby—I really believe that you would have made life very happy for Eleanor. I can't pretend to love you, or even hold out the hope that I could do so in the future—you see, I'm being as honest as you. I think I've forgotten how to love, and I'm not sure that I want to fall in love again—there are plenty of girls around who come easily and go just as easily—perhaps I'm getting too old.'

'You're not even middle aged. Perhaps if you go on looking, you'll find someone.'

'Oh, very likely.' His voice was light; she felt that he was already putting the whole episode behind him and presently would forget it completely. For some reason that annoyed her. The idea of all those girls rankled too. She dismissed it smartly and asked: 'Will Eleanor go back with you—to your home, I mean or does Miss Timmis fetch her?'

'I'll take her back. I have to attend several meetings, all of them in Europe.' He stopped again. 'I suppose that you wouldn't consider going to see Eleanor once she's home again? It would give her something to look forward to?'

'I could go on my way home from Mrs Burns if it's not too out of the way.'

'Tollard Royal—the other side of Shaftesbury, quite close to Peggy, as it happens. Someone can come over and fetch you from Peggy's—perhaps you could stay for the night?'

'Perhaps,' said Deborah cautiously, not to be hurried into an answer. 'I'd like to see her again.'

'Good we can talk about that later.' He took her arm once more and they walked up the drive to the villa, quiet and gleaming in the moonlight. He opened the door and she went past him into the hall which was dimly lit by a candle lamp.

She waited while he locked the door. 'Thank you for a lovely evening. I'm sorry about—about not feeling I can marry you . . .'

'Don't give it another thought, Debby.' He had come to stand by her, now he bent his head and kissed her gently. 'Sleep well, I enjoyed the evening too.'

CHAPTER FIVE

DEBORAH didn't sleep well; no man had ever asked her to marry him before and even though she had refused, it was something to mull over at great length. Just before she finally dropped off she wondered if she should have given such an important matter more thought. She had said no without hesitation ... anyway, she thought sleepily, it was too late to do anything about it now, only meeting him in the morning was going to be a bit awkward.

She need not have worried; when she and the children got down to breakfast it was to find him casually friendly, offhand almost, giving her the faint, half-mocking smile she so disliked. He stayed that way and the days slipped by in a carefree routine of beach, picnics, bathing and pleasant evenings doing nothing on the patio after dinner, and, although Deborah had another day off at the end of the week, there was no offer to take her into Lagos—or anywhere else for that matter. Not that the professor didn't remain friendly; but he was aloof too. Only to be expected, she supposed, probably his pride was hurt, but since he had solemnly assured her with what she considered with hindsight was rather brutal honesty, his feelings weren't involved in the very least, so that left her with the unwelcome thought that he had already dismissed the whole episode from his mind.

Eleanor, on the other hand, hardly let her out of her sight; and when, at the beginning of the third week, the professor announced that he would have to return on the following day to attend some important meeting and that she would be going with him, the child burst into tears and cried so hard that Deborah found herself promising to go and see her before she went home from the Burns family. She felt reluctant about it, for it seemed to her that the sooner she ceased to see the professor, the better it would be. She found him disquieting; she never quite knew what he was thinking or what he would say next; he could be unexpectedly charming and kind and without warning say something cutting. She hoped, quite passionately, that he would be away from home when she went to see Eleanor.

It seemed quiet when they had gone the next day. The twins bereft of a playmate, were peevish and almost unmanageable by turns, Mrs Beaufort without her son's company was plainly miserable, even Mrs Burns, not one to notice anything amiss, remarked on his absence, and confessed herself upset, then persuaded her husband to drive her along the coast to Albufeira, leaving Deborah to mind the children and keep Mrs Beaufort company. That lady, nicely recovered by now, spent the day with them reminiscing about the professor at great length, so that Deborah got to know quite a lot about him. 'Such a clever boy,' Mrs Beaufort confided. 'Brilliant in fact, just like his father. A great pity that his marriage was such a disaster. Too young of course. He needs to marry again for Eleanor's sake.' She shot a glance at Deborah but her face was almost hidden under the sun hat. 'He's still young enough to enjoy life again—family life—I mean. All this travelling is so unsettling . . .' She gave Deborah a second look. 'What will you do when you leave us, my dear?'

'Go home for a week or two, then go back to the

agency and get another job, Mrs Beaufort. I've enjoyed being here though; the twins are darlings and so is Dee; It's been a marvellous holiday.'

Mrs Beaufort gave a delicate snort. 'Hardly a holiday for you, Deborah—three children to care for and precious little time to yourself! but there, I suppose you will tell me that's why you are here.'

Packing up was a sad business even though Deborah did a little here and there so that the children wouldn't notice too much, and on the last day she got up extra early and they went down to the beach in the cool of the morning, parking Dee in her basket where she could see her, and romping in the water with the twins before hurrying back to the house to get ready for breakfast. They left immediately after the meal, and drove to the airport to board their chartered plane and Deborah had no chance to take a last look round, which was perhaps just as well.

They drove back to Ashmore in Mr Burns' car, rather squashed, what with the luggage, Deborah, the twins and Dee on the back seat and Mrs Burns squashed in with them, so that Mrs Beaufort could sit in comfort in front. It was a cool, overcast day and Mrs Burns, usually the most good natured of young women, was disposed to find fault with everything. It was a relief to get into the house and whisk the children up to the nursery to give them their tea and then get them to bed early. Deborah, busy seeing to Dee and then starting on the unpacking, was grateful for the tray of tea Mary brought up to her. She sat drinking it wishing she was back once more by the sea. A silly waste of time, she reminded herself; it had been marvellous but there was no reason to mope about it. She went back to her unpacking.

At dinner, with Mrs Burns cheerful once more, Mr

Burns interrupted himself during a rambling résumé of their holiday to ask: 'You'll stay for a day or two, Nanny? Three or four days just while Peggy adjusts and we get the twins back to Nursery School and everything back in place once more. I'll be home for several months and Mary has a niece in the village who will come every afternoon and take over the children for a couple of hours. It's just a question of getting them settled in again.'

She wanted to go home and tell her mother about the villa and the children and Mrs Beaufort—she might even mention the professor, but she saw that she would have to postpone that for a little longer.

'Yes, of course I'll stay—would four days do? If I could leave on Friday . . .?'

'I'll drive you back, shall we say directly after lunch?'

The four days went quickly; besides coping with the twins: getting them to school each morning, taking them walking in the afternoon with Dee, helping Mary in the evenings after the girl from the village had gone home, Deborah had a mass of small garments to wash, iron, and lay tidily away and since Mrs Burns had the reins of the household to pick up once more, and Mr Burns had to spend a day at the head office of his firm, she spent what free time she had (which wasn't much), by herself. Inevitably, she passed the time mulling over her stay in the villa, wondering about Eleanor, and unwillingly wondering about the professor too. He would be deep in his economics, she supposed, offering other learned men the benefit of his expert advice.

On her last day before leaving Mr and Mrs Burns had gone to dinner with friends and she had her supper on a tray and had then gone to sit in the

nursery to finish the mending before she went to bed.
She had packed, washed her hair and slapped a face
mask guaranteed to turn her into a beauty overnight,
on to her freckled face; so now she sat with her hair in
shining tresses hanging down her back, her beautiful
face unmade-up, plying her needle and thinking. She
hadn't meant to think about the professor, but
somehow sooner or later he seemed to take over in her
head. He would be in Brussels perhaps, or the middle
East or America. She bit off the thread only half
hearing a car stop in front of the house. Where else did
high powered economists go?

Apparently to their niece's nursery, for there he
was, standing in the doorway watching her.

Deborah pricked her finger, muttered under her
breath and said with studied coolness: 'Good evening,
Professor Beaufort.'

He leaned against the wall, looking at her. 'Nanny
back in her safe little nest,' he observed blandly.

'I'm leaving tomorrow,' she told him sharply.

He came a little further into the room. 'Anything in
view?' he wanted to know.

'I hope to have a week or two at home. In peace and
quiet,' she added.

'If that's what you think you'll be old before your
time—who wants peace and quiet until they're
knocking eighty?'

She chose to ignore that. 'How is Eleanor?'

He was all at once serious. 'Missing you. She's
downstairs now with Mary, handing over the apples
we picked for her. Be kind to her, Deborah, she's not
happy.'

Deborah put down her sewing. 'Why not? Does she
miss the twins and the fun we had?'

He shook his head. 'No, she misses you—she'd

rather set her heart on having you for a mother you know. I expect you thought my wish to marry you was for purely selfish reasons, in fact I wanted to make Eleanor happy.'

He shrugged. 'That's water under the bridge, isn't it? But if ever you should change your mind, the offer still stands. In the meanwhile, I hope you'll spend the day with us tomorrow?'

Deborah was on the point of saying that no, she didn't think she could, when Eleanor came in, her small serious face at once alight with joy at the sight of Deborah. It would have been cruel to have refused in the face of the child's pleasure in seeing her again. Deborah returned her hugs and said yes, she'd love to spend the day with them. 'Only you'll have to tell me how to get there,' she pointed out.

'You will be fetched directly after breakfast,' said the professor with faint smugness at having got his own way. 'I'll leave you two to have a gossip.' He added belatedly: 'You ought to be in bed Eleanor.' His daughter took no notice of him, too busy telling Deborah about the four kittens the family cat had produced only that morning.

Deborah was up betimes finishing the rest of her packing, coaxing the twins from their beds and feeding Dee. She had phoned her mother before she had gone to bed and explained that she wouldn't be home until later in the day, cleverly skirting round her mother's searching questions, and now, breakfast over, the twins kissed good-bye and, Dee given a final cuddle, she stood watching the professor's Bentley coming up the drive. It was a vintage car, beautifully kept and probably worth its weight in gold. Eleanor was beside him on the front seat and after a brief flurry of good-byes, Deborah was shoved in beside them, clutching a large paper-wrapped box Mrs Burns had pressed upon her. Her cases had been stowed in the back by Mr Burns and the professor had turned the car and sailed back down the drive before she had had time to do more than wave.

'What's in that box?' asked Eleanor, squashed by her closely, her hand tucked into Deborah's arm.

'I've no idea, we'll have to open it when we get to your home, won't we?'

'Yes, please. You will stay all day won't you?'

'I'll drive you home after Eleanor is in bed.' He spoke so decisively that Deborah, her mouth open to dispute this, changed her mind and said thank you so meekly that he glanced at her sideways and then, very much to her annoyance, laughed.

It was a short drive through country lanes and then up a steep hair pin bended hill. 'Quite rightly named Zigzag Hill,' commented the professor, 'And the view from the top is magnificent, only we won't stop now, Mrs Buckle will be brooding over the coffee pot.'

They came down the hill through a leafy lane with here and there glimpses of the country around them, and came upon Tollard Royal with unexpected suddenness. It was a small village but very beautiful, with a nice old pub, a church, several cottages and skirted by the grounds of a big house where horses were bred, Deborah was informed by Eleanor. There was a scattering of larger houses, well spaced out, but they had gone through the village for perhaps a quarter of a mile before the professor turned the car through an open gateway and slowed along a curved drive bordered by shrubs and trees. The house at the end of the curve was old, red bricked and of a respectable size. It was long and low, with gables, tall twisted chimneys and mullioned windows set in stone frames and its solid, wooden front door stood open.

'Home,' said the professor and got out and went round to open their door. 'Eleanor, take Deborah somewhere where she can tidy herself—we'll have coffee in the sitting room when you're ready.'

A very large buxom woman with boot button eyes in a round cheerful face met them in the hall. 'There you are, dearie, and the young lady with you.' And when Eleanor introduced her to Deborah, with a very correct, 'Deborah this is Mrs Buckle our housekeeper, Mrs Buckle this is Miss Farley!' Mrs Buckle beamed at them both. 'Now isn't that nice?' she asked of no one in particular. 'Just you take Miss Farley up to the Chintz Room, love and I'll take the coffee in.'

She sailed away through a baize door at the back of the panelled hall and Deborah followed Eleanor up the uncarpeted oak staircase, along a gallery and into a room at the back of the house; a charming room, furnished in mahogany decorated with marquetry and living up to its name by reason of the faded chintz curtains at the latticed windows and the matching bedspread. It was a comfortable, luxurious room with an easy chair or two and the glimpse of a bathroom through a half-open door. There were fresh flowers too. Deborah wondered if all the bedrooms had those as a matter of course or whether the professor had been so sure of her coming that he had ordered them to be put there. She bent to sniff at them and then sat down before the dressing table to comb her hair. Eleanor, perched on the bed, watched her.

'It's super having you here—couldn't you stay for a few days? I thought—I wanted you to marry Daddy— I still do. I suppose you couldn't change your mind?'

Deborah turned to look at the child. 'Your father did ask me,' she said, 'but I—I couldn't accept . . .'

'Don't you like him?'

'Oh, yes. Yes I do, but I'm not clever and he is, and I'm not used to all this.' She waved a hand at the elegant furniture around them, 'Besides, I think that people should love each other if they're going to marry.' She paused because after all, Eleanor was only a child still; what would she know about love?

She was surprised when Eleanor said at once: 'Oh, I know about that; Daddy explained, but he said that a lot of people got on very well together without it; he said sensible people like you and him. My mother didn't love Daddy, you know, at least she thought she did at first but she went away with someone else . . . Miss Timmis told me because I asked her one day.' She added matter-of-factly: 'I couldn't ask Daddy, could I?'

'No,' agreed Deborah. And then to change a conversation which was getting a little out of control: 'Is Miss Timmis here?'

'Yes, she's dying to meet you; she says she's longing to be just a governess and not a surrogate mother—she didn't tell me that, I heard her telling Daddy.'

Eleanor slipped off the bed and came to stand by Deborah, 'But if you marry Daddy you'll be a real mother won't you? A nice young one—we could have such fun and I'd help you look after your babies.' The child sounded so wistful that Deborah felt a lump in her throat. If I go on like this I'll be in a fine pickle, she told herself and got up briskly. 'Let's go down,' she invited, 'I'd love to meet Miss Timmis.'

The sitting room was long, low ceilinged and panelled like the hall. There were comfortable chairs and sofas scattered around, several small tables bearing reading lamps and two walls held bow fronted cabinets, but there was still plenty of space. The professor was standing at the end of the room at an open french window with a black labrador beside him gazing out, and sitting nearby was a small, compact lady, very neat with grey hair in an old fashioned bun and wearing gold rimmed glasses fastened by a chain to a pin on her dress. She was so exactly what Deborah had imagined a governess to look like that she smiled involuntarily and Miss Timmis smiled back and got up.

The professor turned round. 'There you are.' His tone implied that they had been a long time away. 'Deborah, this is our Miss Timmis, prop and mainstay of both Eleanor and myself.' He glanced across and smiled at the governess: 'Miss Timmis, this is Deborah Farley, whom I hope to marry sooner or later—preferably sooner.'

He ignored Deborah's indrawn breath and Miss Timmis, taking her heightened colour for shyness, said at once: 'How splendid that will be—such a delightful young wife and mother.' She added in sentimental tones: 'How happy we shall all be.'

Deborah was strongly inclined to point out that she wasn't at all happy and wished for nothing but to be excluded from Miss Timmis's romantic musings, but she held her tongue, largely because the professor was watching her, waiting with wicked anticipation for her to speak.

She smiled and murmured at Miss Timmis, bent to pat the dog's head and observed that the garden looked delightful. A mistake because she was barely given time to swallow her coffee before the professor whisked her outside with the bland observation that, since she found the garden delightful, he would give himself the pleasure of showing her the whole of it. 'While you have your music lesson, Eleanor,' he added and allowed the lid of one eye to drop as he said it. Deborah was quite taken aback with Eleanor's instant agreement; she wasn't looking at Miss Timmis or she might have wondered at that lady's bewilderment.

Contrary to her forebodings, the professor uttered not one word concerning themselves, instead he dwelt at great length on the various shrubs, trees and flowers which made up the very large garden, explaining their Latin names in a kindly fashion which set her teeth on edge. Then, when she felt that the subject should be exhausted, he began on the weeds.

Deborah stopped on a narrow path between beech hedges, instantly vexed with herself for not waiting for a more roomy spot, for her companion, politely stopping as well, was a great deal too close. 'Look,' she said severely, 'I like gardens very much, but I thought I came to spend the day with Eleanor.'

'Oh dear, oh dear, I haven't made much headway, have I? You know—absence makes the heart grow fonder—such a comforting theory. Ah, well. There was no harm in hoping that you'd changed your mind . . .'

'I cannot think,' said Deborah in a carefully matter-of-fact voice, 'why you wish to marry me?'

'I didn't make myself clear? Eleanor needs a mother and you fill the bill, and the only way to bring that about is to marry you, isn't it? We shall get on very well together—you're hardly the sentimental type are you? And I'm not in the least in love with you, although I like you well enough to want to marry you. But it will be a marriage without the romance—I hope I make myself clear?'

'Oh very,' said Deborah in a smouldering voice. 'I wonder if there's a girl in this world who has received a proposal . . .'

'A second proposal,' he reminded her.

'A proposal,' she continued taking no notice, 'so very candid and business-like. I doubt it.' She started to walk on again, 'And the answer is *no*.'

'I felt that it might be. Nonetheless, if you should change your mind will you come to me and tell me so? And I promise you that I won't ask your reasons?' He put a hand on her shoulder so that she had to stand still again and turn to face him. 'Promise?' he repeated.

She studied his face; there was no trace of mockery now, like that she could imagine that he would make a good friend. 'I promise,' she said.

Eleanor came running to meet them as they turned into the drive. She got between them, taking an arm of each. 'Miss Timmis likes you,' she told Deborah and peeped at her father who shook his head slightly. 'She's nice, isn't she?'

'Very. You are lucky to have someone like that to teach you.'

'Yes, aren't I. Will you come and see my room?' She glanced at her father again. 'You don't have to go away Daddy?'

'No, love, but I've got some work to do until lunch time. Shall we meet in the drawing room at half-past twelve? You've a lot to show Deborah!'

He made not another attempt to talk to her alone all the rest of the day and during the drive back to Dorchester he kept up a gentle flow of small talk which left her feeling vaguely resentful.

When they arrived at her home she invited him in, in a polite voice which expected a refusal, but he accepted at once. Instantly at ease with her mother and father, sitting there, she thought crossly, like an old family friend, drinking her father's beer. He was clever at parrying her mother's questions, not evading them merely turning them aside with polite vagueness. He got up to go at length and since it was expected of her, she saw him to the door.

'Thank you for a delightful day,' she told him. 'It was super seeing Eleanor again.'

He paused in the open doorway, put a finger under her chin and lifted it. He didn't say anything at all, only bent and kissed her cheek.

She went on standing there for quite some time after the car had slid smoothly into the evening dark.

It surprised her when she got back to the sitting room, that her mother had no questions; instead she suggested that Deborah might like to go to bed after such a long day. 'And you'll have a few days at home before you start looking for another job, won't you, darling? Professor Beaufort said you'd had a busy time of it even though it was in such a lovely place.'

Deborah had been home a week and had made up her mind to ring the agency the following morning when the agency clerk phoned her.

'I know you were thinking of a permanent post somewhere, sometime after Christmas, but it's only just November and one of our nannies has just phoned to say that she has to go home for a week—her mother's died, poor dear, and she wants to know if there is anyone to replace her just for that time. It's in London—Belgravia—nice house, three children under ten years old and sole charge. To be honest they are a bit of a handful, she says, but it's only for a week . . .'

Deborah, feeling unaccountably restless, didn't give herself time to think about it; she said yes, as long as it was only for a week, and went to tell her Mother. 'I might as well stay at home until Christmas, Mother, if that's all right with you? That will give me time to look around for a permanent post, somewhere where I can stay for a really long time . . .'

'Yes, dear,' her mother looked as though she wanted to say a good deal more than that, but she didn't.

Deborah left for London the next day, she would have liked a few more days at home, even though she had planned to ring the agency; looking out at the city's suburbs crowding in on either side of the train, she had to admit that she didn't know what she did want.

The agency had been quite right, the house was indeed nice—a quite inadequate adjective thought Deborah, getting out of the taxi and looking at its imposing front. Georgian London at its best, three storeys of it gleaming with paint and window boxes. She noticed the bars on the top floor windows—the nursery, well out of the way. She hoped it wasn't the kind of family where the children were kept out of sight all day then allowed downstairs for an hour after tea. She mounted the steps—anyway it was only for a week . . .

She was admitted by a butler with an expressionless face who answered her civil greeting with a voice chilly enough to make her shudder. He led her upstairs to a vast drawing room where the lady of the house was lying on a sofa reading. A quite beautiful woman, beautifully dressed. She glanced up at Deborah, put down her book and said: 'Ah, the temporary nanny. I expect you'd like to go upstairs straight away. The children know that you are coming. Bring them down at half-past five will you? They go to bed at seven o'clock and you will be free after that—they usually sleep all night. Bennett will see that you get your meals in the schoolroom.' She added, not unkindly but with a complete lack of interest, 'I hope you'll be happy while you are with us.'

Deborah, going up more stairs behind Bennett's poker like back, doubted that.

Not only had the agency been right about the house, they were right about the children too; they were just about as difficult as she had ever encountered. At the end of the first day, she wondered if she would be able to stick it out for the rest of the week; she was fond of children but it was hard to like these three: spoilt and rude and ill mannered. Through no fault of their own, she guessed, for they saw their mother for barely an hour each day, and for the entire week Deborah never set eyes on their father. He was in the house all right, his voice often to be heard, even from the fastness of the top floor, but he never came to the nursery. No wonder the children were such little toughs; she hoped that the nanny she was replacing was kind to them.

The week dragged along; Deborah, who found London, even in the bright autumn weather, not a patch on the wide horizons of Dorset, walked the children to the park each afternoon, saw them to school in the mornings, and kept them amused indoors. No one had mentioned off duty to her; she supposed that since she was only there for a week, none was considered necessary.

It was the last afternoon, in the morning she would be leaving the moment the other nanny got back, and she had taken the children to Green Park, wheeling the four-year-old in his old fashioned pushchair, although in her opinion he was perfectly capable of using his own legs. They were waiting to cross Piccadilly when a taxi passed them with the professor sitting in the back. It stopped a few yards further on and he got out, paid off the driver and strode back to where Deborah was still standing.

'The last place I expected to see you,' he observed. 'Rather far from home aren't you?'

He glanced at the children who stared back at him. Deborah was staring at him too. 'So are you,' she said. She found her voice with difficulty, and then went pink because she had sounded rude. 'I mean,' she explained carefully, 'I am surprised to see you here.'

'I get around.' He glanced at the children again. 'These the permanent lot you were so keen on acquiring?'

She said with dignity, 'I am filling in for their nanny; she'll be back tomorrow. I must go—it's time for the children's tea.'

'I'll walk with you.' And he did, the whole way, firing questions at her as she went. 'You'll go back by train I suppose?' And when she said yes: 'The morning, I believe you said?' And when she said yes again: 'Remember it takes the best part of half an hour in the rush hour.' Which led her quite naturally to tell him that she had arranged for a taxi already, 'And it won't be the rush hour; I asked at the cab rank and they said that twenty minutes was heaps of time, besides the eleven-forty's never full and I've got my ticket.'

'A sensible precaution.' He bent his gaze on the child in the push chair. 'Can't this little chap walk?'

'Of course he can. He is four years old; his mother prefers him to be wheeled around.' She spoke in a neutral voice which said a great deal.

'This is where the children live. Good-bye, Professor Beaufort. Please give my love to Eleanor.'

He nodded. 'I certainly will do that. Good-bye, Deborah.' He stood on the pavement and watched until she had ushered her small party indoors. She was filled with vague sadness that he hadn't said a word about seeing her again, although there was no reason why he should, was there?

Naturally, when she took the children down to the drawing room after tea, they told their mother about the man who'd got out of a taxi and walked home with Nanny in an excited chorus. Their mother looked across the room to where Deborah was sitting. 'I should have made it clear, Nanny, that I don't allow followers unless you have a free day.'

Deborah clasped her hands tightly together. She said very evenly: 'Professor Beaufort is the brother of Mrs Burns, whose children I've been looking after, he was kind to enquire why I was in London. And I have no followers.'

If the coldness of her tone was noticed, it wasn't remarked upon, but: 'Professor Gideon Beaufort? A charming man, I met him recently at some party or other. Such a pity—he could have come in for a drink. Oh, well—you can take the children, Nanny. Nanny Masters is back in the morning, isn't she? Come and see me before you go and you can collect your wages.'

How could anyone so beautiful to look at be so rude, thought Deborah, herding the three children back to the nursery, supper and bed.

Nanny Masters arrived soon after breakfast, a thin stern woman in her forties, who waved away Deborah's tentative sympathy and wanted to know if anyone had remembered to make appointments with the dentist for all three children.

'Well, I haven't for nobody asked me to,' said Deborah, her usually mild temper slowly inflaming at Nanny Master's pointed remarks about hair needing cutting and why was the four year old wearing grey socks with blue knickers. 'Unless you want to talk about anything else, Miss Masters, I'll go—I have a train to catch.'

She said good-bye to the children which was a waste of time, and as for Nanny Masters her lips parted in an even thinner smile. 'I daresay you'll be quite good at your job when you've had my experience.'

Deborah bit back rude words, muttered and went to her room. She was still in uniform and there was no time to change. She buttoned herself into her uniform coat, planted the no-nonsense hat on her sandy head, and went to collect her wages, handed over with a casual good-bye and no thanks.

Well, it didn't matter, she could forget her unpleasant week and the money was welcome. She picked up the case one of the maids had carried down to the hall, and since there was no one about, opened the door and hurried down the steps.

The professor, sitting in his vintage Bentley, leaned over and opened the door and then got out and took her case, throwing it on to the back seat he shoved her gently into the front seat.

'I'm going by train,' protested Deborah. She had been unable to put up any kind of resistance to his large hand in the small of her back, but she sat upright, looking ready to spring out of the car at any moment.

'No,' said the professor, 'I'm driving you down to Dorchester. I'm on my way home.'

'Not if you go to Dorchester, you're not.'

'What I like about you, Debby, is your habit of not mincing your words. Now just relax and put up with the inevitable.'

He drove in silence for some minutes. 'Was it very bad?' he wanted to know.

'Pretty awful. I think that the children weren't loved

enough. I never saw their father although he was often in the house—he didn't come near the nursery and they spent an hour with their mother after tea each day. No wonder they were so anti.'

'Poor little blighters. What is the nanny like?'

'Stern and unbending, she disapproved of me. Isn't Eleanor with you?'

'No, I'd like to have her with me, but what would the child do all day while I'm tied up with work. If we were married of course, it would be different, you would come too and that would solve the problem.'

Deborah said faintly: 'There is Miss Timmis . . .'

'Who has no interest in window shopping or Madame Tussaud's or standing for hours outside a church were there a wedding to see. I can't say I blame her at her age. Now you—you're younger and would enjoy such things.'

'You don't give up, do you?' observed Deborah in her severest voice.

'No I am glad you realise that. Let's stop for coffee.'

They had their coffee in a wayside pub and drove on. 'We should be back in nice time for lunch, that is if your mother lunches at half-past one.'

'One o'clock. Would you like to stop at a phone box and I'll ask her to wait until we get there.' She added belatedly: 'Will you stay for lunch?'

'I was beginning to think that I wasn't going to be asked.'

Whatever Mrs Farley's plans had been for the meal she had done wonders in the short time she had had. The cold joint had been ruthlessly minced, and was now a mouth watering cottage pie, Mr Farley's early sprouts, just ready, lay piled in a dish and when he caught sight of them and opened an indignant mouth, he was silenced by a fierce look from his wife. Even the last of the cherished greenhouse tomatoes were on the table. Later he would have something to say about that, but now he greeted their guest politely, offered him a drink, engaged him in conversation and presently sat down to table.

The professor enjoyed his meal and complimented Mrs Farley with such charm that she blushed. 'Do have some more sprouts,' she urged him, 'my husband grows them you know—he's a keen gardener.'

Which gave him the happy cue to discuss gardening in all its aspects with his host. Deborah, almost silent, watched her father's carefully concealed annoyance evaporate and winked at her mother, who gave her a little smile and a nod. When there was a pause in the conversation she asked: 'You'll stay home for a little while, love? You haven't said much about these last people, but I don't think you enjoyed it much, did you?'

'Not really. Yes, I'd like to stay at home for a bit.' She looked defiantly at the professor, who smiled gently and raised his eyebrows. She looked away quickly and he said: 'I really must be going; I promised Eleanor I'd be home for tea. A delightful meal, Mrs Farley.'

He shook hands, leaving Deborah to last, and letting her hand go almost before he had clasped it. She stood at the porch watching him get into the car and fought a fierce desire to nip into the seat beside him. She wanted to go with him, more—she wanted to stay with him. She never wanted to let him out of her sight again, and if this was love it was simply terrible, swamping one at a most awkward moment when it was quite impossible to do anything about it. The sensible thing to do would be to call him back and tell him that she'd changed her mind, but for one thing she was having difficulty with her breathing, and for another, one simply didn't do things like that. Why couldn't she have discovered it on their drive down? She could have brought the conversation round to marrying him in a cool and collected way, and never let him know that she had fallen in love with him. One thing she knew: she would marry him. It would be difficult but not impossible to be the kind of wife he wanted, and surely she could be happy even if she did have to hide her love?

She followed her parents indoors and did the washing up in a dream, hardly conscious of her mother's cheerful talk; and presently, when she went upstairs to unpack, she sat on the bed instead and allowed dreams, quite impossible dreams, to take over.

CHAPTER SIX

DEBORAH remained in a state of euphoria for the rest of the day, but with morning came common sense. She hadn't changed her mind about marrying Gideon Beaufort—indeed her wish to do so was stronger than ever, but there was no use in pretending to herself that there was going to be any romance about it; that didn't mean to say that she wouldn't make a success of it. He wanted a mother for Eleanor and someone to fill the place of a wife even if he had no wish to get involved romantically. She dared to think that they might become good friends; he had said that he liked her and that was important and she loved him enough to want him to be content and free of worry about Eleanor. And miracles did happen. Who knew? He might, in time, fall a little in love with her.

She thought about it all the next day, presenting a *distraite* manner to her puzzled parents and then, in the evening, asked her father if she might borrow the car.

'Why?' asked Mr Farley.

It was as good a time to explain as any. 'Well, Gideon has asked me to marry him—several times, and I've always said no, but I've changed my mind, and I promised him that if I ever did so I would go and tell him. So I thought I'd drive over to Tollard Royal tomorrow.'

'Can't you phone him?' asked her father.

Mrs Farley said sharply: 'Really, Tom, that would be most unsuitable. You're quite sure, darling? He's a good deal older than you are, though I must admit that he is a remarkably handsome man, and should make a good husband.' She added by way of explanation: 'Nice manners, you know.'

Deborah didn't say anything and her mother went on: 'You haven't known each other very long, have you? Not that that matters; one can fall in love at first sight, and no one need tell me otherwise.'

Neither of her companions contradicted her and presently Mr Farley said: 'You would live at Tollard Royal, I suppose?'

'Yes, Father, but Gideon would like us—Eleanor and me—to go with him sometimes when he has to attend these conferences.'

'H'm—well, Debby, you are old enough to know your own mind and you've shown you're sensible enough to know what you want. Go and talk to Beaufort, but I hope that he'll come and see me.'

'I'm sure he will, Father. And may I take the car?'

'Yes, certainly.' He hesitated. 'You'll be happy with him, Debby?'

She turned a suddenly happy face towards him. 'Oh, yes, Father. I'm very sure of that.'

She left soon after breakfast and drove without hurry, taking the smaller country roads. She had dressed with care in a dark green velvet jacket, a tweed pleated skirt and a cream silk shirt with a pie-frill collar. Her high heeled shoes were on the seat beside her because she couldn't drive in them, but she would change the elderly lace-ups she was wearing when she reached the house.

It was a crisp day, but the sun shone and the country was at its autumnal best; her spirits rose as she drove, she was going to see Gideon again and that was all that mattered.

The village looked charming as she drove through it and presently turned in to the grounds of his house. The brickwork glowed in the hazy sunlight and there were a great many windows open, but the front door was closed. Deborah drew up carefully before it, got out and pulled the old fashioned bell. Mrs Buckle answered it almost at once.

'Well, I never—Miss Farley. What a surprise. Eleanor's at her lessons but the professor's in his study working. Come in and I'll let him know you're here. Lucky that you came when you did, for he told Buckle he wanted the car after lunch.'

She steamed across the hall with Deborah at her heels, but before she could tap on the study door Deborah said diffidently: 'Mrs Buckle, would you mind very much if I surprised him? I . . .'

The boot button eyes twinkled at her. 'Of course not. It'll be just the thing, he's been sitting over his papers far too long for the last day or two.'

Deborah waited until the housekeeper's vast form had disappeared kitchenwards, then knocked on the door and went in.

'I don't wish to be disturbed,' observed the professor without bothering to look up.

'Well, yes—I suppose I should have phoned you first but if I had you would have wanted to know why I should want to see you and I couldn't explain over the telephone.'

He put down his pen and got slowly to his feet. 'Forgive me, Deborah—I wasn't expecting you. What can I do for you?'

His voice sounded friendly but hardly encouraging, only she had made up her mind and she wasn't a girl to change it again. 'I don't think you can do anything for me,' she told him. 'It's me that can do something for you. You asked me to promise to come and see you if I ever changed my mind. Well, I have, but if you don't want to marry me I'll quite understand . . .'

'Why should I not want to marry you?' He was quiet, smiling a little.

'Well, people get fed up with waiting for answers, don't they? And I've said no several times.'

'Indeed. And why have you said yes now, Deborah?'

'You said you'd not ask me my reasons.' The fright in her face sent his eyebrows up, but all he said was: 'You're quite right, I did say that. I won't ask a single question and I still want to marry you.' He added lightly. 'Shall I propose again, just to make sure?'

She said seriously: 'Oh, no there's no need. There's just one thing—I'm not marrying you because you're rich, I mean I'd still marry you if you were poor. I've thought about it and I expect having a lot of money will make it much easier, won't it?—you'll be able to go off to wherever you go and leave Eleanor and me here.' She stopped when she saw the thunderous look on his face, drew a breath and finished bravely: 'That's what you intended wasn't it? For me to look after her while you were away?'

'A masterly summing up, Deborah. You have the situation in a nutshell. Eleanor will be delighted, and so for that matter, am I.' His mouth twisted in a wry smile, 'I should have said that sooner, shouldn't I?'

She said in her sensible way: 'No, why should you? If we're to be friends then we mustn't pretend, must we?' She blushed brightly as she spoke because, of course, her whole life was going to be one long pretence from that moment.

'Most sensibly spoken. When shall we marry? There's no reason to hang around is there? I don't suppose you want to glide down the aisle in white satin, do you?' His eyes were fixed on her sandy locks and then studied her face, and the blush which was beginning to die down took fresh fire.

She lied in a firm voice. 'Oh no, nothing like that, but I would like to marry in church and I'd like my family and some of my friends to be there.'

He said carelessly: 'Why not? I'll get a special licence—shall we say in three weeks' time? Two weeks if you could manage it; I have to go to the Hague and we could take Eleanor with us—you two can amuse yourselves while I am working.'

She tried to make her voice as businesslike as his and succeeded very well. 'What a splendid idea. Two weeks will be ample time. Will you make the arrangements—we go to the parish church . . .'

'We had better go together, hadn't we? We'll settle the details presently, I think. In the mean time shall we tell Eleanor?'

She was sure of one thing, Eleanor was happy which helped to warm the rather chilly feeling she had inside her; it was going to take a great effort to remain as cool and offhand as Gideon, but she promised herself that she would cope. If she had patience he might discover that he loved her—she was a great believer in miracles. In the mean while she returned Eleanor's ecstatic hugs warmly, received Miss Timmis's delighted good wishes and accompanied Gideon to the kitchen, so that he could tell the Buckles.

By then it was lunchtime and it was while they were having their drinks that Gideon observed it might be a good idea to phone her mother. 'I should of course, like to have a talk with your father,' he pointed out, and picked up the phone on a side table.

'I told Mother and Father why I was coming here,'

said Deborah quietly, 'I said I'd be home around tea time.'

He smiled at her. 'I'll drive back with you in my own car.' He dialled and in a moment said: 'Mrs Farley—Deborah is here to speak to you,' and held out the phone.

Mrs Farley took the news with considerable calm, expressed her delight, agreed to tell her husband when he got home for lunch and invited Gideon to supper. 'You'll have a good deal to talk about,' she declared, 'and two weeks isn't long.'

'No, Mother,' said Deborah, 'we'll talk about that when I get home. Here's Gideon.'

She had to admit that he said exactly the right things; she pictured her Mother's pleased satisfaction as she rang off, she had known for some time that although her mother loved her dearly, she had never entertained much hope of Deborah getting married. She had been told bracingly so many times that she would make a splendid wife, and she thought, without conceit, that she would, but men liked a wife, however splendid, to have a modicum of good looks too. A good hairdresser, thought Deborah and she would splash out on one of the expensive brands of make up. But what to wear? It was an awkward time of year . . .

'What's worrying you?' enquired Gideon. It was a casual question and she answered just as casually: 'Nothing important,' smiling carefully. 'Clothes and things.'

She saw his faintly mocking smile and said quickly to Eleanor: 'What would you like to wear at the wedding, Eleanor?'

'May I be a bridesmaid? And wear a blue dress . . . oh, please . . .'

'I'd love that if your father allows it?'

'Of course she may—make whatever arrangements you like, I'll have to leave a lot to you, I've two or three important meetings coming up. Get what you need and send the bills to me.' He sounded impatient, and Miss Timmis, who had been basking in the reflected rays of a romance right under her nose, looked taken aback. But of course, the dear professor was a very busy and important man and couldn't be expected to waste his time bothering about the details of the wedding. She said in her precise voice, 'I think a navy blue dress and jacket—so useful during the winter months, too.' She caught Deborah's surprised eye: 'For myself you know.'

Deborah was about to enlarge on the interesting subject of weddings when she glanced at Gideon and saw the faint boredom on his face. She said briskly: 'What a good idea; we must have a talk about that sometime! And then: 'I interrupted your work, Gideon, I expect you want to be left in peace to get on with it when we've had lunch.'

She met the annoyed blue eyes squarely and after a moment was relieved to see him smile. 'I see that you will make me an excellent wife, Deborah,' he observed. 'Shall we have lunch now? I'll join you for tea and then we can drive back to Dorchester?'

The dining room was charming and the table beautifully appointed; Deborah ate her lunch, trying to stifle the excitement that in a few weeks' time she would be sitting opposite Gideon at that very table—probably she would have arranged the flowers . . . She was a little *distraite* throughout the meal but Eleanor was too excited to notice, Miss Timmis put it down to being in love and the professor, having got things all his own way, didn't notice either, not because he was excited but because he wasn't all that interested. He had attained his objective; Deborah would make an excellent surrogate mother for Eleanor, run his house with no fuss, be capable of dealing with any small crisis which might arise during his absence from home, and be a pleasant companion without becoming tiresomely starry eyed. He made a mental note to get her a ring and studied her across the table. A nice little thing, no beauty, but a good hairdresser could do things to that sandy hair and she had lovely eyes. He made another mental note to arrange for her to have a generous allowance.

He went back to his study after lunch and became immersed in his work and didn't think of her once.

Deborah being taken on a second and more detailed tour of the house by Eleanor, was unaware of his thoughts, of course, although she was sensible enough to know that to him this marriage was to be a strictly business-like arrangement. It was a little daunting, she mused, stopping to admire some ancestral portraits on the upstairs landing, but she was quite sure in her own mind that loving him as she did would be sufficient to overcome that in time. In the mean time, living with him in his home was the next best thing; she had every intention of being a good wife and she could see no reason why she wouldn't be.

Tea was a pleasant meal, and Miss Timmis listening to the light hearted talk, beamed approval; young love, she thought, disregarding the fact that the professor was no longer a young man, and presently she stood with Eleanor waving to the happy pair as they drove off, Gideon in the Bentley, Deborah in her father's car.

They stopped for coffee at Sturminster Newton and Deborah, naturally dying to talk about their wedding, didn't mention it. A sensible decision which reaped its own reward, for presently Gideon asked: 'You are happy about the arrangements? I'll put a notice in the Telegraph and you had better invite whoever you want to come. We shall go straight over to Holland, so see that you wear something you can travel in. Eleanor seems bent on being a bridesmaid, but I suppose she can cover her dress with a coat.'

Deborah refrained from pointing out that it was already November and the child would wear a coat in any case. As for herself, if he thought she was going to turn up for her own wedding in sensible tweeds, then he was sadly mistaken. She murmured an agreement and sat looking at his hands on the table: large, well cared for and very capable. Her eyes slid up to his face, very good looking although the mouth was firm to the point of hardness, but she liked his faintly beaky nose and his grey hair. Very distinguished, they would make an odd pair she reflected.

Presently they got back into their respective cars, the Bentley held in check behind Deborah's steady pace. She could imagine Gideon's suppressed impatience but there was nothing she could do about it; it was a narrow, winding road and her father would never forgive her if she so much as scratched the paint.

She stopped at length outside her home and the Bentley purred to a halt behind her. Gideon got out and came to open her door. 'You drive well,' he observed. 'I must get you a car of your own.'

She lifted her green eyes to his. 'Really? How super—something small ... I drive faster than this you know, but it's Father's car.' And then: 'You mustn't feel that you have to give me things, you know.'

His blue eyes were very cool. 'Allow me to be the best judge of what I give you, Deborah.' He turned away as the door opened and her mother came out to meet them.

She had been feeling nervous about the evening, but her fears had been groundless. Gideon didn't put a foot wrong; after he had gone home, with the three of them sitting over a pot of tea, Mr Farley pronounced himself quite content with his future son-in-law. 'A sound man, and clever, not boastful thank heaven, but very sure of himself. He'll make you a good husband, Debby.'

'So good looking,' murmured Mrs Farley. 'I'm glad he's bringing Eleanor over to see us, he's obviously very fond of her. You've not had time to talk about the wedding, I suppose? I know we've talked it over this evening, but only in general terms. Two weeks' time— that isn't long—clothes, and we must have a reception even if it's to be very quiet. I wonder if we'd better hire a room?'

'Gideon suggested that we keep the guests to a minimum—we could manage twenty or a couple of dozen people here, couldn't we? We have to leave very soon after the wedding, anyway, he has to go to *den Haag* and Eleanor and I will go with him.'

'Eleanor?' began her mother and then changed it to: 'He's a busy man, I'm sure, it'll be nice for you to have company while he's at these meetings.'

Two weeks was very little time in which to organise even the quietest of weddings, Deborah spent most of the next day making neat lists of things to buy and people to invite. Then in the evening, unexpectedly, Gideon arrived.

'We might go out to dinner,' he suggested, 'there's still a good deal to talk over and while you are getting ready I'll see if your parents are free to come over and spend the day on Sunday. I'd like them to meet

Eleanor. Will you stay for a day or two? I have to go up to London for a few days and it would give you the chance to get used to the place and arrange about Eleanor's clothes. Miss Timmis has a friend who makes Eleanor's things, perhaps if you bought whatever you want for her, she could make it up.'

He glanced rather impatiently at her sensible grey flannel skirt and matching sweater. 'I daresay she would be only to glad to make something for you, or perhaps you'd prefer to buy ... There are some decent shops in Salisbury, or so Miss Timmis tells me.'

She gave him a smouldering look. 'Perhaps you have some suggestions about the colour I should wear?' Her voice was sweet with a nasty edge to it.

'Oh, lord—have I upset you? But since you ask me—how about a rich clotted cream—a fine wool dress and a matching coat. If you have your hair decently dressed and some sort of a hat you'll be quite attractive.'

She said in a voice which trembled: 'You seem to know a great deal about it, but I think I should warn you that I'm not a doormat by nature and you may find it harder than you think to change the ways of a rat trapped gorgon. I like to make up my own mind, especially about clothes.'

They were standing by his car, for she had been in the garden when he had arrived, now he took her by the shoulders and made her face him.

'Oh Debby, I'm sorry. And your mouth isn't a rat trap; it's a kind, generous mouth. As for being a gorgon, you certainly don't turn me to stone; you give me a nice, warm friendly feeling when I'm with you. I think that with a little give and take, we shall get along very well together.'

Deborah registered a silent promise to wear cream wool. 'I shall do my very best,' she assured him and was surprised when he bent and kissed her quite hard. 'Friendship sealed with a kiss,' he informed her gravely and put his hand into his pocket. 'I hope this fits—it was my mother's. It's old fashioned because it was my grandmother's too. Try it on.'

He took the ring out of its box and slipped it on her finger, and she stared at it with delight; it fitted perfectly—that must be a good omen. It was a sapphire surrounded by diamonds and set in gold; she touched it gently. 'It's beautiful Gideon. Thank you very much.' She would have liked to have cried, but she made her voice friendly and nothing else.

They went indoors and the ring was duly admired before she went to change; she stood for quite some moments in front of her small wardrobe, wondering which dress Gideon would like. In the end she settled for a russet wool, by no means the height of fashion but the colour suited her. Not that it mattered, she told herself, applying make-up with care, he had a low opinion of her dress sense. She would have liked to have experimented with her hair, but there wasn't enough time. 'If only I had some sort of a hat,' she told her reflection and giggled.

They went to the Old Market House in Cerne Abbas, and ate the delicious food at leisure. Deborah had never been sure if she liked champagne, but now she decided she did; perhaps because she was given more than one glass and the champagne was a good one. She remarked that it was a very pleasant drink and Gideon smiled slowly. 'In the right company there's nothing like it.' He waited while she was served pears cooked in red wine and smothered in cream.

'Now, as to the details of the wedding—shall we get them settled?'

It had been a very pleasant evening, she thought sleepily, getting ready for bed; she had, she considered, matched his casual friendliness very well; discussing the wedding as coolly as though it were not her own, but some acquaintance's. They had agreed on almost everything, and she had accepted the life he had outlined for her without demur. A pleasant enough prospect, most of it at Tollard Royal—the quiet country life she enjoyed, with occasional visits to Shaftesbury or Salisbury, his friends to entertain, and the house to run with Mrs Buckle to guide her. He would be home for the most part of the time, he had told her, but occasionally he had to stay in London and whenever possible there was no reason why she and Eleanor shouldn't be with him. And when he had to go to Brussels or *den Haag* or any other European capital not too far away, there was no reason why she, and perhaps Eleanor too, shouldn't accompany him. He had been very matter-of-fact about it and even for a few moments she had wondered if she would be able to go through with it, but of course she could; she loved him and that was surely the best reason in the world for marrying him. And having settled this she closed her eyes and slept.

She had told Gideon that two weeks would be ample time in which to get everything arranged for the wedding, but she hadn't reckoned on the time taken up by his surprisingly frequent visits, the dinner party he gave at his home, with the Burns and Mrs Beaufort, and they in their turn giving a dinner party in return. Besides, the boys were home for half term, hindering her at every turn, talking excitedly about the wedding. And then there was Eleanor's dress to see to—the pair of them spent the day in Salisbury searching for exactly the right material—sapphire blue velvet and a matching tweed coat to go on top of it. That done and safely delivered to the dressmaker, she at last got down to the task of finding something to wear for herself. She found it in Sherborne, in a small, expensive boutique where normally she wouldn't have dreamed of going. But just for once, and quite forgetting that when she was married she would be able to buy all the clothes she wanted, within reason, she felt justified in being extravagant. It was not only the exact shade of cream she had in mind, it also fitted perfectly; a simply cut dress in fine wool with a top coat of thicker tweed. The price paled her cheeks, but didn't prevent her from buying a little blue velvet hat the colour of Eleanor's dress and then adding shoes, gloves and a handbag. She was just about flat broke by the time she got home, but she had what she wanted.

They were to be married at half-past eleven, have a buffet lunch at her home, and leave directly afterwards for Holland. Since Gideon had the car with him they would cross by Hovercraft and drive up through Belgium along the coast road, to reach *den Haag* in good time for dinner.

Mrs Farley, happily immersed in plans for the reception, deplored the fact that it had to be such a quiet affair, although, as she assured Deborah, that didn't mean to say that it wasn't going to be an extremely elegant one. As for Deborah, all she could think of was that in a few days' time, she would be Gideon's wife.

She was up early on the morning of the wedding, contrary to custom pottering round the house, helping her mother get breakfast, arranging flowers, polishing glasses, and finally going back to her room to get herself dressed. She was sitting before her dressing table mirror, carefully doing her hair in the style the hairdresser had suggested. when she heard Eleanor's excited voice. A moment later there was a tap on the door and the child came in.

'Deborah ... Oh, don't you look nice, and your hair's different, is my dress all right? Daddy liked it. He's gone to the church, but he left your flowers. They are downstairs ...'

Deborah gave her a hug. 'You look smashing, and see, I found a hat which matches your dress. Just sit still on the bed while I put it on.' And when she had done so: 'How do I look?'

'You're beautiful,' declared Eleanor and she meant it. Deborah thanked her soberly; it would be marvellous if Gideon thought the same, and still more marvellous if he were to say so.

There was, of course, no opportunity for him to say anything at all when they met, but the long look he gave her as she joined him at the end of the aisle gave her a pleasant glow; at least he approved of her appearance, and since she had taken a considerable time to achieve it, she was satisfied. The glow lasted all through the short service and turned her into what Mrs Buckle, there with Buckle, described as a radiant bride. Mrs Buckle was a sentimental lady and saw the occasion through rose coloured spectacles, but all the same Deborah bore all the outward signs, at least, of a very happy young woman. The dear professor looked happy too, she declared, though happy wasn't perhaps the right word; his handsome features bore an expression of satisfaction—he had got what he wanted; a mother for his small daugher, and a wife who gave every indication that she would fall in with his life-style and refrain from indulging in romantic ideas.

What was more, he liked her; she was a good companion and she had a mind of her own. No looks, although he had to admit that there was something about her which caught the eye . . .

Deborah, sitting beside him in the Bentley being whisked off to the Hovercraft, admitted to herself that he had behaved beautifully, he had the easy good manners which made him liked by everyone and he had called her his dear wife when he had made a brief speech after they had cut the cake. She believed him, he might not love her, but she was sure in her bones that he thought of her as a companion and a friend.

She peeped sideways at his profile, impassive and silent and had her thoughts interrupted by Eleanor's excited voice from the back seat, still intent on discussing every aspect of the wedding. A topic which kept them fully occupied for the greater part of the journey.

Neither Deborah nor Eleanor had been on a Hovercraft before. Gideon, who had, answered their endless questions with good humour and patience and once they had landed, kept up a casual running commentary of the country they were passing through. Once over the border, he turned off the motorway and stopped at an hotel in Rosendaal where they had tea and fragile little biscuits. Deborah, who had hardly eaten any breakfast and almost nothing at the reception, would gladly have gobbled up a plateful. As it was, she nibbled at them daintily and hoped that no one could hear her insides rumbling.

The professor, watching her, smiled faintly. 'I think that when we get to the hotel, Eleanor had better go straight to bed and have her supper there, otherwise she will not enjoy your morning together.'

She was an obedient child and agreed placidly. 'Will you be working all the time?' she asked her father.

'A good deal of it, I'm afraid. But I'm sure the pair of you will find more than enough to do. The conference I have to attend is being held near the hotel though I doubt if I shall get back for lunch, but I think we might all go to the puppet theatre one evening, and to Scheveningen for Sunday lunch. There's a splendid zoo and an ice skating rink if you skate, Deborah?' And when she nodded: 'Good, I can see that you will both be amply amused. And, Eleanor, sometimes I shall take Deborah out in the evening and you will have your supper in bed and one of the chamber maids will look after you. Okay?'

Eleanor nodded. 'Will you go dancing?'

'I daresay we shall. We shall certainly tell you all about it afterwards.'

He signalled the waiter. 'Shall we go? It's not much further now.'

Deborah found *den Haag* to be a very elegant place, she admired the broad, tree lined avenues, and the solid houses lining them. Then as they neared the heart of the city, the brightly lit shop windows and old fashioned trams and the crowded streets. Gideon drove without hesitation, finally turning into Lange Voorhout, and parking before the Hotel des Indes. Its foyer was comfortable and a little old fashioned, but the service was instant and unobtrusive. She knew very little about hotels, but she guessed that this one was in the luxury class and when they reached their rooms she found this to be right, each elegantly furnished and with a splendidly appointed bathroom too, with communicating doors so that Eleanor, who was in the middle, could go into either room if she wanted to.

Deborah unpacked for them both and when Eleanor went to see her father, she went to her own room and tidied herself. Presumably they wouldn't be going out that evening, so there was no need for her to change her dress. Presently Eleanor came back and Gideon with her.

'Shall we go down and have a drink, and get a menu so that Eleanor can decide what she wants for her supper, then she might go to bed, don't you think? When she's settled perhaps you will join me in the bar again?'

The three of them went downstairs and found the bar crowded, but Gideon sat them down at a table near one of the windows, and ordered lemonade for Eleanor and drinks for Deborah and himself, then laid himself out to be entertaining. It wasn't until Eleanor had finished her drink and decided what she wanted for her supper that Deborah suggested the two of them might go back to their rooms to which the child agreed readily. It had, after all, been a long and exciting day.

It was half an hour or more before she was in bed, her supper tray on the bed table. 'I'll come back to see that you've eaten it,' promised Deborah, 'and tuck you up.'

Eleanor beamed at her. 'It's so nice to have a mother. Will you tuck me up every night?'

'Well, of course, darling, I expect that Daddy will too when he is at home.'

She watched Eleanor start off on the food and then went down to the bar, feeling shy. She found Gideon standing with several men, deep in talk, but when she came in and he saw her, he broke off what he was saying and came to meet her.

'Eleanor settled?' He wanted to know. 'Most of the

commission seem to be staying here, come and meet some of them.'

He took her arm and steered her through the crowded room and introduced her to a handful of men, all older than he, some Dutch, some English. They were charming to her and although she felt a little out of her depth she did her best and was rewarded presently by Gideon's: 'Well, you did very well, Debby. You look so pretty in that dress too.'

'Not pretty,' she told him sharply, 'you know I'm not that.'

He said frankly: 'I've never thought of you as pretty, but I see that I was mistaken—you've done something to your hair . . .'

She looked away. 'The hairdresser showed me how to arrange it.' She glanced around her. 'And the light's dim in here.'

He laughed then, not unkindly, but all the same it hurt. He went on: 'Shall we have dinner—we can dance if you like.'

'That would be nice. I'll just see if Eleanor's all right, I promised I would tuck her up.'

'How easily you have fallen into your new role,' he smiled and got up with her. 'I'll come too.'

Eleanor had eaten her supper and was sitting up in bed reading. 'Bedtime,' said Deborah firmly and took the book away with a smile. 'You can wake me up in the morning if you like . . .'

'Ah, yes, I'll arrange for morning tea. Half-past seven? We don't start until ten o'clock, but I've some notes to make first—if we could have breakfast at half-past eight?'

They said good-night and went downstairs once more to the restaurant and were led to a table in the window, not too near the small dance floor. Deborah studied the menu. 'I could eat everything on it,' she observed, 'I'm famished.'

'Me too. Let's see—shall we have lobster soup? I think I'll settle for a steak, but I'm told the *poulet a l'estragon* is excellent—would you care to try it?'

The sharp edge of their appetites blunted by these delicious foods, they danced before going back to their table to enjoy soufflé Harlequin and then they danced again. Deborah was a good dancer, shedding her rather prim appearance once the music started, and Gideon, who for years had only danced when it had been unavoidable, was agreeably surprised.

'For an ex-nanny, your dancing is quite astonishing. Did you dance for one of those T.V. dance groups on your days off?'

She said severely: 'Certainly not, when would I have had the time?' She added thoughtfully: 'It would have been fun, though, I do like dancing.'

'I am rapidly coming to the conclusion that I like dancing too. We must indulge our liking as often as possible, Deborah.'

They lingered over their coffee and it was almost midnight when Deborah went up to bed. Their good-night was formal as they were in the restaurant, and she was glad of that, anything else would have had her on the verge of tears. 'And what else did you expect,' she muttered to herself as she undressed. 'Be thankful for what you have got and make the most of it.'

She frowned at her forlorn face in the mirror and got into bed. She had often dreamed of her wedding day, what girl didn't? But she had never imagined that it would be like this. 'It doesn't matter,' she mumbled to herself, her head buried in the pillows. 'I love him—I have to remember that, and I've got years ahead of me to make him love me.' She closed her eyes and presently two tears squeezed their way down her cheeks. It was all very well to have years and years in which to do that, but she couldn't think how to set about it. She had no beauty with which to charm him, she would learn to dress well in time, but at present there was nothing about her to catch the eye. She considered herself rather a dull companion, especially for a man such as Gideon. Really all that she was fit for was to be a mother to Eleanor, and that after all was why he had married her. He had never minced matters over that.

But she felt better about it in the morning; Eleanor and her early morning tea arrived together and a few minutes later, Gideon joined her, sitting on the side of the bed and eating the tiny sweet biscuits which had arrived with the tea. It was all very cosy and domestic and a splendid start to the day. And what a day; at the end of it, with a tired but happy Eleanor tucked up in bed, Deborah lay there in the bath and thought about it. They had seen very little of Gideon, but then they hadn't expected to; he had left them soon after breakfast but not before giving her a street plan, a phone number to ring if anything went amiss, and a fat roll of notes. Her eyes had almost popped out of her head when she had counted them.

The shopping streets were close by the hotel, the two of them had made their way there as soon as Gideon had left them and wandered up and down the arcades, looking in all the windows and finally going into La Bonnetiere to find a dress for Eleanor; dark red taffeta and just the thing for Christmas. After that it became imperative that Deborah should buy herself something too, and since the roll of notes was still comfortably thick, she bought a pleated chiffon dress over a silk slip, it had long tight sleeves and a deep V neckline, so it showed off her pretty figure to advantage. 'Shoes,' prompted Eleanor so that slippers had to be searched for and bought, plus a purse which matched exactly added to the parcels.

They had stopped for coffee, purchased a bead necklace Eleanor fancied and then taken a tram towards Scheveningen, got off at Madurodam and spent a fascinating hour touring that miniature city, watching the tiny cars and buses travelling through its streets, the ferries in the harbour and listening to the music coming from the church and the opera house. Deborah was just as entranced as her companion and since they had spent far longer there than they had intended, they took a tram back to the city centre and had lunch in a coffee shop; giant pancakes, glasses of milk and enormous cream cakes. Deborah had thought that had Gideon been with them he would have had something to say about unsuitable diets, but it was exactly what they had both fancied and had revitalised them sufficiently for them to pay a visit to the Ridderzaal, where they trailed behind a guide and a dozen or so other people, trying to take in all that they were being told.

'I liked the morning best, shopping,' Eleanor had said as they went back through the Binnenhof, past the Vijver pond and made for the hotel. It was almost tea time and Gideon said that he would be back to have tea with them.

He was there, waiting for them and she had been relieved to see that he did no more than raise an amused eyebrow at their parcels and ask if she needed more money for the next day. She had assured him that she had plenty to spend still and sat quietly while Eleanor had poured out the excitements of the day. Only when she had finished did she ask: 'And you, Gideon, have you had a good day?'

She had been taken aback at his abrupt answer; he didn't want to discuss his work, or perhaps he thought that she wasn't interested, for he started a lively argument with Eleanor about the evening's programme; bed, he said firmly, there was another day tomorrow and he would book seats for the puppet theatre. 'You can amuse yourself this evening?' he asked Deborah, 'I've quite an amount of work to do and one or two people I've promised to meet.'

She had said quietly that yes, of course—she had letters to write and a book she had bought that morning and was dying to read. The hope that they might have been going out somewhere that evening where she could have worn the new dress, she buried deep inside her. He hadn't wanted to know what was inside their parcels and probably her lovely dress would never be worn. Tomorrow she decided, applying careful make-up, they would go to the Mauritshuis because it was one of the places he had suggested they visit, and then they would go shopping again, this time for an outfit which she could wear each and every day and they would dash back to La Bonnetiere and get the fur lined gloves Eleanor had wanted.

She had been surprised when there was a knock on the door and Gideon walked in. 'Eleanor's settled? You've arranged for her to have supper up here?'

Deborah laid down her powder puff. 'Yes, I did wonder if we might have dinner together, just the two of us, but I thought you might not like that. But I shan't be long over dinner and I've promised her I'll read to her when I get back.'

He leaned against the dressing table, looking down

at her. 'My dear Deborah, do I detect reproach in that remark? I explained to Eleanor before we came that she would only stay up for dinner on one or two occasions. Now if you are ready, shall we go down?'

She had put on one of the dresses she had bought before they married; not particularly fashionable but pretty. She stood up now, hoping that he would at least notice that she was wearing something different, but he went to the door and held it open for her without a word.

She drank her sherry talking nothings to the same men she had met the previous evening and ate her dinner without appetite. As soon as she had finished her coffee, she said in a cool voice: 'I will go back to my room now, you must be wanting to—to do whatever you want to do. Goodnight, Gideon.'

He got up with her and followed her out of the restaurant and walked through the foyer to the stairs. He halted there while she teetered, on the lowest tread, not wishing to be impolite but wanting to go.

'You haven't told me about your day,' he observed blandly. 'Did you buy anything interesting?'

'Eleanor told you about her dress.'

'And you?'

'Oh, I bought a dress too.'

'And lunch—where did you go?'

She gave him a guilty look. 'Well, it was quite late by the time we'd looked round Madurodam. We went to one of those coffee shops in the arcades—we had pancakes with bacon in them, milk to drink and chocolate cakes with whipped cream.'

He gave a subdued shout of laughter, bent his head and kissed her hard and suddenly, wishing her goodnight he walked away, leaving her looking guiltily round to see if anyone had noticed. The foyer was almost empty and nobody was looking her way. Perhaps he'd had too much to drink, she mused going slowly upstairs, but upon reflection she knew that to be absurd. She reflected with satisfaction that she hadn't kissed him back although the temptation had been great. The less she thought about the whole episode the better; she hurried to Eleanor's room and began to read the 'Wind in the Willows' in a calm, quiet voice.

CHAPTER SEVEN

THE second day was as good as the first, better in fact, for Deborah found a wool jersey separates outfit in a green which exactly matched her eyes. The price made her shudder, but trying it on she was instantly aware that it did something for her. Her hair lost its sandy colour and became pale auburn, her eyes shone like emeralds and the cut of it turned her from mundane dowdiness into instant chic. She and Eleanor marched out of the shop their hearts light, and her purse even lighter. Not so light, however, that she wasn't able to purchase a hat to go with the new outfit, and in an exactly matching shade of green; a ridiculous trifle which when perched on her neat head transformed it immediately to the very pinnacle of fashion.

They had their elevenses, bought the gloves and a fur cap for Eleanor and then mindful of Gideon's instructions once more, went to the Mauritshuis where they gazed at the Rembrandts, Vermeers, Jan Steen and an enormous canvas by Paulus Potter—the bull—they retraced their steps to study it for a second and third time, bewitched by its size and its lifelike style.

Eventually Deborah said with reluctance. 'We really must go,' and added: 'We'd better have lunch at the hotel, your father didn't quite approve of our meal yesterday.' She blushed as she said it, remembering how he had kissed her. 'At least I don't think he did.'

They had their lunch and then went to Deborah's room, where she tried on the green outfit and the hat while Eleanor sat on the bed watching her, her fur cap on her head, the new gloves in her hand. Deborah was rotating slowly and a little anxiously, craning her neck to see the back.

'Is it a bit tight?' she wanted to know and heard Eleanor giggle and then Gideon's:

'Certainly not—it's—er—a most pleasing fit.' And when she whisked round to stare at him: 'I didn't startle you? this afternoon's meeting has been adjourned and I came back here on the chance of finding you.'

He came further into the room and deliberately turned her this way and that. 'Delightful—who would have thought ... Keep it on, Deborah, such an attractive outfit deserves a new top coat.' He turned to his daughter. 'Get your coat, love, we'll go shopping.'

'We've been shopping most of the morning,' said Deborah faintly. 'At least we did go to the Mauritshuis ...'

'Splendid, that leaves us all the more time to shop now.'

He bustled them out of the hotel and towards the shops, where presently in the cathedral calm of a very select boutique, Deborah found herself trying on coats in tweeds, fine wools, cashmere ... she chose a rich chocolate brown cashmere. She had tried to see the price on its label but Gideon said softly: 'No, Deborah, there is no need for that.' A remark which made her blush rosily. She supposed that in time she would buy things without bothering to look at their price and with female logic she chose a beret thrust through with a quill, which the saleslady assured her was intended to be worn with the coat. She stared at her reflection in the large mirror finding her image almost unrecognisable; this highly fashionable woman staring back at her didn't seem to be her at all, she looked, well, not pretty but certainly worth a second glance.

But Gideon merely glanced once, his 'very nice', was to her ears, decidedly tepid. She swallowed disappointment and said in a bright voice: 'May we buy Eleanor a dressing gown? We saw such a pretty one this morning—it was in one of the arcades . . .'

So they went in search of that before having tea in an elegant little tea shop and then going back to the hotel to dine early and go to the Puppet Theatre. Eleanor sat entranced and so did Deborah; Gideon hardly looked at the stage but watched their faces, his own was impassive.

They stayed for two more days, into which they crammed enough sight seeing to satisfy the most seasoned of tourists. Indeed they enjoyed the tour of the city's canals so much that they went a second time, this time with Gideon for company, and on their last day Deborah took Eleanor to the Costume Museum, where they inspected bygone fashions and spent a great deal of time poring over the dolls houses before shopping for presents to take home. Eleanor was allowed to stay up for dinner on their last evening and pronounced it to be the best holiday she had ever had, didn't Deborah agree?

Deborah said serenely: 'By far the best—it's been wonderful, though I'm sorry that your father had to work so hard.'

'No need to waste pity on me,' declared Gideon carelessly, 'I daresay I should have been bored with nothing to do.' A remark which left his daughter quite unmoved and to which Deborah took the greatest exception.

She said chattily: 'I expect you'll be glad to get home again?'

'Yes, although I shall have to be in London for several days at a time.' He was watching her narrowly. 'But I'm sure that you will be able to fill your days.'

Deborah didn't answer, but Eleanor said at once: 'Oh, yes Daddy, there's heaps to do—I'll never be lonely again now we've got Deborah. Miss Timmis said how nice it will be just to be a governess and concentrate on teaching me things. She doesn't like long walks you know, or swimming or going shopping . . .'

Her father laughed. 'I can see that Deborah is going to lead a strenuous life. Now how about going to bed, love?'

Deborah got up at once and an attentive waiter pulled back her chair as Gideon got to his feet too. 'I'll come up with you,' she began and was interrupted by his: 'But come down again, won't you? I thought we might dance for a while?'

They danced for a long time and when Deborah suggested that she would go to bed she had been reminded with gentle blandness that they were, after all, on their honeymoon.

He had looked at her with a small mocking smile as he spoke and she wasn't sure if she wanted to hit him or burst into tears, instead she said brightly: '*Den Haag* is such a lovely place for a holiday, though I expect you know it well.'

'Next time we come we must go further afield; I've had several invitations for us both to visit associates here—some of the old country houses are charming.'

The band paused so they went back to their table where Gideon ordered another bottle of wine. 'Miss Timmis had a talk with me last week—she has an older sister who is a semi-invalid and she very much wants to visit her. Could you cope with Eleanor for a few weeks on your own? She has no intention of leaving us, but she also suggested that Eleanor might like to go to school now that she has a more secure background, and that she might stay on as a general factotum, sewing and so on,' he added vaguely.

'Of course I can cope,' said Deborah briskly. 'Is there a good school nearby?'

'Oh, yes. If you could drive her there and fetch her . . . I thought that perhaps after Christmas . . .'

'Will she like that?'

'I think so—of course we'll talk to her about it. There will be people coming to stay during the next week or so—old friends, people I meet at work, now that I have a wife it will be easy to entertain them at home. I shall bring them back with me at the weekends.'

'I see, will you be gone all the week?'

'Not every week.' He gave her a thoughtful look. 'Debby, are you happy?'

She said instantly, 'Oh yes, indeed I am. It's all a bit strange, of course. I mean, all this . . .' she waved a hand vaguely around her, 'but I do my best, Gideon and I'll get better.'

'My dear, you're everything I could wish for in a wife and Eleanor loves you.'

But you don't, thought Deborah silently, and if I were clever I'd know how to make you love me, only I'm not clever and I'll just have to hope that you will or that something happens to make you.

They travelled home the next day, a smooth journey that went without a hitch, to be met by the Buckles' welcoming faces, great log fires in all the rooms and an elegant dinner. Eleanor, who had chattered away unceasingly all day, was almost asleep by the time they had finished and Deborah whisked her off to bed.

'Miss Timmis will be here in the morning,' she pointed out, 'wanting to hear all about our holiday and you don't want to fall asleep in the middle of telling her.'

Gideon got up and opened the door for them. 'Come down again Deborah,' he said, 'we must have a talk.'

Now what, thought Deborah as she urged Eleanor into her bed and tucked her up, half throttled by the child's arms.

When she joined Gideon in the drawing room, Buckle had brought in the coffee tray and put it on a small table by a chair drawn up to the fire opposite Gideon. It looked cosy in a grand way, and she thought sadly how delightful it would have been if Gideon had leapt to his feet and kissed her, just as a newly wedded husband would. He certainly got to his feet but he showed no signs of kissing her, merely invited her to sit down and pour the coffee.

'I'll have to go to town tomorrow,' he observed as she handed him his cup, 'and I probably shan't be back for a couple of days—it's hardly worth the journey home since I have to attend another conference on the second day. I thought we might have our first guests next weekend; they can drive down with me on Friday evening—I'll let you know who and how many, and we might give a dinner party before Christmas, don't you think? You'll need some clothes—you might leave Eleanor with Miss Timmis and come up to town with me—let me see——' he frowned a little. 'If I drive down on the day after tomorrow you could go back with me in the morning, but you may have to take a train home—you'll go to Salisbury and Buckle can pick you up there.'

She murmured her agreement; there wasn't much

point in doing anything else, he had obviously decided it all for himself. He went on: 'That will give you a day in which to make sure that everything is all right for the weekend.' He glanced at her: 'Mrs Buckle will help you; she knows where everything is and Miss Timmis is a tower of strength.' He smiled suddenly: 'Although I imagine that you are quite capable of arranging a weekend for any number of people without turning a sandy hair.'

He hadn't meant to be unkind she told herself, but she, who had \been enjoying rising self assurance engendered by her new wardrobe, became instantly aware of that same sandy hair and ordinary face. She said soberly: 'I expect I can manage. I'll come up to town with you if you wish . . . what shall I need? That is—are your friends smart?'

'The women? Well yes, not outrageously I suppose, but good, well cut clothes and pretty dresses in the evening—you know?'

She wasn't sure that she did, but she nodded. It was very humiliating that he so obviously didn't consider that the clothes she had were good enough. Why on earth had he married her? She knew the answer, of course, because he loved Eleanor and wanted the child to be happy; all the same, it was a pity that he couldn't have settled upon a chic beauty who combined a high sense of fashion with affection for Eleanor. She sighed without knowing it, and he said sharply: 'You're tired, go to bed it's been a long day.' He got up and opened the door and as she went past him touched her lightly on the shoulder. She paused and smiled at him and wished him good-night, crossed the hall and went upstairs. He watched her go . . . she was a graceful girl. He waited until she was out of sight before going back to the drawing room, reminding himself that he would have to go to his study and go through his post, but he went on sitting there, staring into the fire, his thoughts unaccountably given over to Deborah; he wasn't thinking of her suitability as a wife but of her wide green eyes and her sandy hair—beautiful hair actually—shining with cleanliness and good health; in her new green outfit she was quite something. He realised suddenly that given time to acquire poise and in the right clothes, she would be a knock-out. And of course, she was splendid for Eleanor; he had chosen wisely. He got up presently and went along to his study, to sit down at his desk. He found it quite an effort to start on his letters, but of course, once he did, he dismissed her from his mind.

The next morning, sitting opposite her at breakfast, he hardly looked at her and when he did, it was with the tolerant eye of a friend; certainly there was no vestige of glamour about her at eight o'clock in the morning. She was wearing a sweater and a skirt and her hair had been brushed smoothly back and pinned up quite ruthlessly. She looked fresh and wholesome and very young. He put down his post and asked mildly: 'What are you two going to do today?'

'Well, Miss Timmis comes back after lunch and Eleanor's got such a lot to tell her so if you don't mind, since it's so early, I thought we might drive over to Dorchester . . .'

'A good idea, take the Mini. Give my love to your mother. We must arrange a visit very soon.' He smiled at her. 'I must be off; I'll be home tomorrow early evening. Don't forget you are driving back with me.'

He got up and came round the table, stopping to kiss Eleanor on the way. At Deborah's chair he stopped again. 'Why do you screw your hair up like that?'

'It's quick.'

He leaned forward and pulled the pins out of her hair so that it fell loose round her shoulders. 'That's even quicker, and much prettier.'

He kissed her slightly open mouth and went away, leaving her a little pink and Eleanor giggling.

She wore the new green outfit and the coat Gideon had bought her, when they left presently in the Mini; her mother's surprise at her new image gave her deflated ego quite a boost. 'Darling!' declared her parent, 'you're positively pretty—and your hair . . . does it take ages?'

Deborah nodded, 'But once it's up it stays that way.' She plunged into an account of their trip to *den Haag*, handed over the presents she had brought with her and then sat quietly while Eleanor babbled excitedly.

Just before they left Mrs Farley asked: 'You're happy, darling?'

'Yes, Mother,' Deborah kissed her and added, 'Very.'

Miss Timmis arrived after lunch and Deborah left Eleanor and her together while she went to the kitchen to talk to Mrs Buckle. She didn't know how many guests Gideon would invite, but she could at least talk things over with the housekeeper. They spent an hour or more deciding on which rooms to get ready and possible menus, by then it was tea time. She spent the evening with Miss Timmis, finding that lady's gentle talk very soothing. All the same she was glad to go to bed; the house without Gideon seemed very large and empty, even the dogs were subdued.

Eleanor had lessons in the morning and Deborah spent it in inspecting the various bedrooms and then making a list, with Mrs Buckle's help, of food they might need to get in. There was a well stocked, large larder and a freezer too; Buckle knew all about the wines and the greenhouses were nicely full of chrysanthemums and pot plants. There wasn't much more that she could do, so she spent a pleasant afternoon in the library while Eleanor had her music lesson then the three of them had tea round the schoolroom fire with Deborah glancing every five minutes at the clock. Gideon would be coming soon, the dogs knew it too sitting in a heap on the hearth rug.

Five o'clock struck and after what seemed like a very long time indeed, six o'clock. It was half an hour after that when the phone rang and Deborah went to answer it on the schoolroom extension before Buckle could get to the phone in the study. Gideon's voice, casual to the point of coolness, came very clearly over the line.

'I'll not be home until about eleven o'clock,' he told her. 'Old friends have asked me to dine—don't wait up for me, I'll see you at breakfast. Let me speak to Eleanor will you?'

Deborah said nothing at all, she put down the receiver and called to Eleanor, then went to sit down again by Miss Timmis and started to talk rather loudly so that she wouldn't be able to hear what Eleanor was saying. The child came back presently, she looked resigned. 'Daddy says he met Auntie Barbara while he was having lunch—he asked her to come for the weekend, but she isn't sure so he is taking her out to dinner instead.'

'Lady Barbara Inge,' murmured Miss Timmis. 'Married one of the professor's friends—they are divorced now. A very beautiful young woman. She has been in America I believe.' She glanced at Eleanor's downcast face: 'You'll see your father in the morning, Eleanor.'

Deborah made an effort. 'Yes, of course, love. I'm sorry you are disappointed, we all are. Shall we have a game of cards then you can have your supper and Miss Timmis and I will have dinner at the usual time. I'd better let Mrs Buckle know.'

Why, she pondered on the way to the kitchen, should Gideon tell her that he had been asked to dine with old friends and yet be doing nothing of the sort? He must be feeling guilty or surely he could have told her the truth—or perhaps he thought it was none of her business? It was a lowering thought.

They had their game of cards and while Eleanor ate her supper with Miss Timmis for company, she took the dogs for a walk. It was a cold, dark evening, exactly suited to her mood and she walked fast, trying to get away from her thoughts. But it didn't help; she went down to the village and back again, took the dogs into the kitchen for their supper and went back to the schoolroom. Eleanor had just finished her supper and Deborah said cheerfully: 'Since Miss Timmis will have you all day tomorrow, how about me seeing you to bed?' She smiled at the little lady, 'Do go down to the drawing room and give yourself a drink: I'll be with you shortly.'

She pottered round the child's room while Eleanor undressed and then went to run her bath. 'It's a pity that Daddy's not here,' said Eleanor, 'I wanted to tell him about my history; Miss Timmis says I'm very good at it—I wanted to surprise him.'

'Think what a nice surprise it will be in the morning,' observed Deborah, 'and I'll tell you what, you shall stay up for supper tomorrow evening—I'll ask Miss Timmis to get you all ready for bed and you can wear your new dressing gown!'

A happy thought which sent the little girl to bed content.

Miss Timmis went to bed happy too; dear little Mrs Beaufort had listened with sympathy when she had explained about visiting her sister, indeed, she offered help if it should be needed and expressed pleasure in knowing that Miss Timmis would return in the role of a family companion. Miss Timmis's small frame swelled with pride at the nice things which had been said to her. The professor was a very lucky man to have such a sweet natured girl for a wife.

Deborah, neither happy nor in bed, sat by her bedroom window with the lights out staring out into the dark. She had never imagined that being married to Gideon was going to be easy, but she hadn't expected him to be so indifferent; it would have been better if she irritated him or made him angry, as it was she did neither. She would have to do something startling; go blonde perhaps? buy some really way out clothes that even he couldn't ignore? develop a semi-invalid condition which would allow her to lie around all day in frilly negligees—go home to mother?

She giggled and then choked on the tears crowding her throat. Sitting and moping wouldn't do any good at all; she had married Gideon with her eyes open and she would make a success of their marriage although just at that moment she couldn't think how. She sat by the window until she saw the car's lights as it came from the village and then got into bed, still in the dark.

She was her calm, serene self in the morning, chattering gaily to Eleanor about her shopping, promising to bring her a present, letting her sit on the bed, which she enjoyed, while she did her hair and face. She had decided to wear the green again and the new coat and beret, they went down to breakfast in good time with Eleanor still talking nineteen to the dozen.

Gideon was already there reading his mail, his breakfast pushed to one side. He pushed his chair back as they went in, but Deborah said quickly: 'No don't get up, Gideon. I hope you don't mind, I told Miss Timmis to come down later.' She served Eleanor and herself and started to sit down, while the little girl went to kiss her father. He looked over his daughter's fair head: 'Why?'

'Well, it's early, isn't it? and she will have Eleanor all day. She'll be here by the time we go.'

He ruffled Eleanor's hair. 'What a good idea,' he sounded absent minded, thinking of other things. Aunt Barbara perhaps, wondered Deborah and bit savagely into her toast.

She said with careful casualness. 'I hope you had a pleasant evening with your friends,' and hurried on before he could reply: 'We played cards and Eleanor won—she's good you know, Miss Timmis and I never have a chance.'

He wasn't in the mood for small talk. 'You'll be all right if I drop you off at Harrods? Take a taxi to Waterloo when you've finished your shopping. I suggest that you phone Buckle from there and he'll meet you. Don't stint yourself, Deborah—your allowance is in the bank, and if you go over it ask for the bill to be sent to me.' He mentioned a sum which sent her pale eyebrows up into her hair.

'All that?' she asked incredulously.

He said smoothly: 'You can fit yourself out for the next month or so.'

She thanked him, she certainly would do that; she would let herself go, and outshine his women friends.

The drive to London was totally taken up with

details as to the guests they might expect that weekend. 'We don't do much; walk the dogs, and perhaps ride if the weather's good, sit around and chat. I'm sure you will be able to lay on a good dinner each evening; Mrs Buckle is a first rate cook and is always complaining that she has no chance to show her talents to the world. Miss Timmis will help you with the flowers and the linen and so on.'

He was driving fast, looking ahead, and Deborah, seething silently at his assumption that she was quite out of her depth, said nothing.

'Well?' His voice was impatient and faintly annoyed.

'I'm sure that everything will be all right. You must tell me if I do anything wrong or fall down on my duties, but I don't imagine that your friends will expect a polished hostess, considering the circumstances in which we married.'

He made an explosive sound which she took to be a swear word she wasn't familiar with. 'Do you imagine that I broadcast my—our—personal lives to every Tom, Dick and Harry I meet? I have no doubt at all that you will be an excellent hostess.' He added to surprise her: 'I'm sorry if I was overbearing.'

'Not at all. If there's anything special about your guests will you tell me? So that I know what to talk about.'

'A pity we can't meet for lunch—I have a previous engagement and I can't get home this evening either. I shall bring two of our guests with me—he's something in the E.E.C., very quiet and easy to talk to, so is his wife. Then there will be another married couple; he works with me a good deal, rather learned and withdrawn, his wife is just the opposite—they're a devoted pair. Then there is another guest—a last minute one—which makes us an odd number but that can't be helped. An old friend just back from the States . . .'

'Aunt Barbara,' murmured Deborah.

He drove in silence for a few moments. 'Eleanor told you?'

'That's right,' her voice was matter-of-fact although her heart was pounding with a mixture of quite murderous feelings. 'Did you think that she wouldn't? And you could just as well have said so to me in the first place; why should I mind about your friends? After all I know almost nothing about you, do I?' She took a breath, 'And I'm not a bit interested.'

He didn't reply, although when she peeped at him she could see his profile was taut and severe; she had annoyed him and she was glad. After that they didn't speak again. He stopped outside Harrods and she thanked him for the lift, smiled emptily at his chin because she didn't feel quite able to look him in the eye, and walked jauntily into the store.

The jauntiness dropped off her like a cloak once she was inside and she shook so much that she went first to have a cup of coffee. She hadn't done well, in fact she had behaved badly. How easy it would be, she thought, if they could talk—really talk, about themselves. He had put her into a compartment; she was a small part of his life, a convenience not meant to mingle with his own way of living, but to live in his home, run it to his liking and love his daughter. In all fairness, she had known that when she had married him, and if she hadn't loved him so much she might have thought the situation through and backed out.

She finished her coffee and got out her list. Well, she wasn't beaten yet and she would change her tactics . . .

Having money yourself to spend was a great help;

she chose greens and browns and rich tawny shades—
tweed suits beautifully cut, cashmere sweaters, silk
blouses, an armful of fine wool and silk dresses and
three evening gowns, all very much in the fashion. Six
months ago she wouldn't have dreamed of even trying
them on even if she had had the money. There was
plenty of money still, she found shoes which cost the
earth, leather handbags and belts, gloves and undies
and, true to her promise, a splendidly dressed doll for
Eleanor and a mohair stole for Miss Timmis. She had
shopped steadily without stopping for lunch and she
was finished by three o'clock. She arranged to collect
her parcels presently and went in search of a tea room.
She wasn't hungry but a pot of tea was what she
needed. She would find somewhere quiet and sit for
half an hour, her train didn't go until five o'clock so
there was time enough. There was a tea room across
the street; she had a foot off the kerb when she saw
Gideon and a tall, handsome young woman crossing
towards her. She had time to compose her features
into a casual smile which almost killed her before they
came face to face. Gideon's face was a blank mask.
He stopped and the young woman stopped too.
'Deborah . . .'

She managed a beam. 'Hullo—can't stop—I've a
train to catch.' She switched the beam on to the girl
and nipped across the street, dying to look back, but
instead she went to the tea room and resolutely took a
table well away from the window. She sat there
drinking cup after cup of tea until she felt better and
then went back and collected her packages, got into a
taxi and caught her train in comfort, sitting alone
surrounded by all the clothes she had bought. They
won't be a waste, she told herself fiercely, they'll help,
I know they will. They'd better; the girl had been

lovely and her clothes quite something. Deborah, her green eyes glowing, marshalled her new outfits in a mental parade like soldiers going into battle and when she had done that to her satisfaction made a note to call the hairdresser in the morning.

Buckle was waiting for her; he loaded her mass of boxes and packages into the car, expressed the hope that she had had a good day, and drove her home. 'The professor phoned just before I came away, Madam, wanted to know if you were back and said he'd try and ring again later.'

She received the news with mixed feelings; if he was going to try and explain over the phone then she wasn't going to listen, on the other hand if she didn't answer when he rang he might think that she was annoyed. Annoyed—she was so angry that she could have burst into flames.

She doused her temper for Eleanor and Miss Timmis's sake; they seemed so glad to see her and so happy with the presents she had brought them. They had supper together and then Deborah undid her boxes and tried everything on before an admiring audience. She was twirling round and round in the finest of her evening gowns when Buckle came to tell her that the professor was on the phone and she went to the extension by the bed. Strangely, she felt quite light hearted, largely because the dress she was wearing had turned her from an ugly duckling into a swan. As Miss Timmis had remarked primly, it was a ravishing dress, even if rather revealing. 'Although as you are a married lady, an exposed bosom is quite allowable,' she had observed.

Deborah perched on the side of the bed with a great rustle of wide skirts. 'Hullo there,' she greeted him and allowed her gaze to sweep over the lovely things spilling over the chairs and bed.

Gideon's voice sounded so cool that she shivered. 'Deborah? I shall be home tomorrow at about six o'clock, Dr and Mrs Wallis and Barbara Inge will be with me, John and Joyce Morris will be arriving half an hour later. We could perhaps dine at eight o'clock. Eleanor had better be ready for bed and I expect Miss Timmis to join us.'

She said airily: 'Okay, Gideon. Eleanor's here, she wants to say good-night.'

'You enjoyed your day?'

'I had a marvellous time, here's Eleanor.'

Deborah was dressed and ready for Gideon and their guests by half-past five. She had spent the day making sure that everything was just so, taken the dogs for a walk so that they wouldn't bother Gideon the moment he came in, and now, dressed in a green crepe dress the exact colour of her eyes, she was sitting in an upright chair, terrified of disarranging the artlessly simple style the hairdresser had created with her sandy hair. Eleanor was with Miss Timmis, getting into her blue velvet dress under that lady's eye, for Deborah had decided that even if the child couldn't stay up for dinner, there was no reason why she shouldn't be downstairs to greet her father, besides that would give Miss Timmis time to get into the navy blue dress.

Eleanor came into the room presently, her fair hair beautifully brushed, her small face beaming with excitement. She walked all round Deborah taking in every exact detail and finally pronounced her to be utterly super.

'Thank you, darling, and remember when I say so, go upstairs, have your supper and get ready for bed.

I'll pop up to say goodnight. Dinner's not till eight o'clock, so I can nip along while everyone is in their rooms.'

Eleanor asked wistfully: 'Do you think Daddy will come too? He always does when he is at home.'

'Then he'll come this evening.'

'I like it better when there's just you and Daddy and me, and Miss Timmis, of course.'

'Yes, love, but Daddy has to entertain his friends and they won't be coming very often at the weekends.'

It was a little after the hour when the Bentley swept up to the door closely followed by a Mercedes. Deborah went into the hall with Eleanor just as Buckle opened the door, she would have much preferred to have run upstairs and shut herself in the fastness of her room, as it was she went forward looking, she devoutly hoped, welcoming. Gideon had stood aside to usher the others in and when he did turn round she was pleased to see the look of astonishment on his face, it was only there for a moment, but it satisfied her; the wildly expensive dress and the hair do had served their purpose. He had really looked at her, he had discovered, she was sure, that she wasn't 'Nanny' any more.

She said in her pleasant voice: 'Hullo, Gideon, did you have a good journey down?' She smiled at him and then at the others.

He crossed the hall and bent to kiss her cheek. For the sake of appearances, she told herself silently as he introduced Dr and Mrs Wallis and then John and Joyce Morris who had come with him after all. 'And this is Barbara Inge—an old friend, just back from America.'

'And utterly devastated to find Gideon married,' said that young lady. 'You see what happens the moment my back is turned?' She looked at everyone, gathering laughs. 'I never was more surprised . . .' She kissed the air an inch from Deborah's cheek. 'He's quite a handful, my dear, but I daresay you'll cope.'

Deborah said sweetly: 'I shall do my best. It's delightful to meet his friends. Do please come in, I expect you would like a drink before going to your rooms?'

Eleanor was talking to Gideon and she led the way to the drawing room as Buckle took coats and hats, and Gideon followed with Eleanor. And from then on a kind of magic mantle fell on Deborah; she had been terrified of entertaining Gideon's friends because she knew nothing about them, come to that, she didn't know much about him, either. But a kind of recklessness had seized her and that, coupled with the knowledge that she really looked rather nice, had the effect of turning her into the perfect hostess, laughing and chatting and what was better, listening more than talking, so that the two men, finding her such a good listener, would have monpolised her if she had allowed it. But she won over their wives just as easily, while Eleanor kept close to her, sipping her lemonade and every now and then tucking a hand into Deborah's. Of course, that left Gideon with Barbara which in a way was very satisfactory, for Barbara was a young woman who liked an audience and the only person attending to her was Gideon, while Deborah, stealing a look at him from time to time, thought that he was bored.

Eleanor said her goodnights presently and after a while everyone went to their rooms leaving Deborah and Gideon together. She sat herself down by the fire. 'I'd love another sherry before you go,' she told him. 'I like your friends, Gideon, are they all as nice?'

He brought her the sherry and stood looking down at her. 'I believe so. You look different, Deborah.'

She said kindly, 'I'm still me, only without the cap and apron.' And then, because he looked suddenly ferocious. 'I didn't want you to be ashamed of me.'

'That is a very silly remark, you must know that you look delightful and that Ben Wallis and John are falling over themselves to get at you. I feel as though I've married a quite different girl . . .'

'Don't you like me?'

He said silkily: 'Oh, indeed I do—I am enchanted—but it would hardly do for me to behave like John and Ben, would it. I am—surprised . . .'

'I am a bit surprised myself, I mean, feeling quite different just because I'm wearing a model dress and have had my hair done differently. But I'm still me.'

She finished her sherry and he took the glass from her and drew her to her feet. 'I think that there is a lot more to you than I imagined,' he observed slowly, 'and I don't mean new dresses and elaborate hairstyles.'

He bent suddenly and kissed her, but this time it wasn't a light peck on her cheek. 'I'm going to change.'

CHAPTER EIGHT

THE weekend was a success, indeed Miss Timmis pronounced it a social triumph for Deborah; nothing had gone wrong—the food had been above reproach, the weather had been fine for the time of year, so that everyone could get out of doors and for those who were disinclined to do that, there were cheerful fires, plenty of books to read and of course, the T.V. Deborah playing her part, avoided Gideon as much as possible, electing to stay at home with Joyce Morris when everyone else went walking on Saturday morning and then offering to show Ben and Mary Wallis the church after lunch. 'And I'll take Eleanor with us,' she said cheerfully to Gideon, 'then if you want to play bridge you won't be interrupted.'

This had been naughty of her; Gideon loathed bridge. When she got back rosy cheeked from the cold, a Gucci scarf exactly matching her beautifully cut tweeds tied under her chin, she sensed a distinct atmosphere at the card table. Gideon looked impassive, the Morrises tolerantly amused and Barbara Inge furious. She turned towards them as they trooped in and said peevishly: 'There you are—I hope you had a better time than I have—Gideon doesn't even bother to play . . .' She flung the cards down and went over to the fire.

'It's cold and lovely outside,' said Deborah lightly: 'We enjoyed it. Just give us time to take our outdoor things off and we'll have tea.'

Sitting behind the teapot presently, Deborah looked

157

around her: The Wallises were enjoying themselves, so were the Morrises, tucking into buttered muffins and one of Mrs Buckle's fruit cakes, so was Eleanor with Miss Timmis sitting beside her. She had personally settled them there so that it was left to Gideon to sit with Lady Barbara.

That evening, after an excellent dinner, she had suggested dancing in the drawing room and the lovely silk rugs had been rolled aside while she selected a few tapes. She was sure that Gideon hadn't wanted to dance, but he had agreed pleasantly enough, filling glasses and joining in the light hearted talk and when she had switched on the tape she had excused herself, explaining that she wanted to say goodnight to Eleanor. Gideon opened the door for her and then went straight across the room to Joyce Morris and started to dance. Deborah, out of the corner of her eye, saw Barbara's cross face, and felt a pleasantly wicked wave of pleasure at the sight.

Everyone left after lunch on Sunday and Gideon had taken Eleanor and the dogs for a walk, suggesting smoothly that Deborah might like to rest. A remark she took instant exception to, although Miss Timmis, going thankfully to her room to put her feet up, remarked upon her employer's thoughtfulness. Left to herself Deborah mooned around the house, picking up the Sunday papers and putting them down again, moving vases of flowers from here to there and back again, finally putting on her old mac and the thick shoes she kept for pottering about in the garden, she let herself out of the back door. She wandered round for a bit and finally took herself off to the shed where Willy the gardener stored the apples. It was cold but fragrant inside, she perched on a pile of old sacks and selected one of his best Cox and bit into it. The weekend had been a success, she felt sure, but Gideon hadn't said a word and yet he had appeared to have enjoyed himself. They had all gone to the village church that morning and she had sat with Eleanor between them in the family pew, and he had smiled at her several times during the service. Probably for the benefit of the congregation, she thought sourly, biting into another of Willy's apples.

She was roused from her thoughts by Gideon's voice on the other side of the house and a moment later all three dogs had hurled the shed door open and were scrambling all over her, just as though she had been away for years.

She felt quite guilty when Gideon and Eleanor poked their heads round the door to look at her. She nibbled the last of the apple core and got up.

'Did you have a pleasant walk?'

'Lovely. Deborah, Daddy says you're a super hostess and there's no reason why we shouldn't have people staying each weekend, only we are not going to because he likes peace and quiet.' Eleanor came close to Deborah and put an arm round her neck. 'I do too, just us. May we play Scrabble after tea?'

'If your father would like that . . .'

'Her father will be delighted, it will make a nice change from bridge.'

'Oh, well yes. Though I should have thought that you would have liked that—I mean you have to be clever to play, don't you?'

He said silkily: 'There are a great many games one can play where cleverness doesn't count, only low cunning and guile.'

She had the grace to blush and jumped to her feet. 'Let's go indoors and have tea. The Buckles have the afternoon off so I'll get it.'

In the hall Gideon said: 'Eleanor, will you go and ask Miss Timmis if she would like tea in her room—I'm sure she would like a good rest.' And when the child had skipped upstairs: 'I'll give you a hand with the tea things.'

'Please don't bother, Buckle will have left everything ready.'

She need not have spoken for he took no notice but followed her along the stone passage to the large, cosy room with its scrubbed table and old fashioned dresser and the kettle simmering on the Aga. The tray was indeed ready but he made no effort to carry it away, instead he sat on the edge of the table and watched Deborah warm the pot and put the muffins to toast.

He leaned across and cut himself a slice of cake. 'A very successful weekend,' he observed, 'we must find time to do it again one day. We can, of course, have Barbara down on her own . . .'

Deborah, measuring tea into the pot, spilt some of it on to the table. 'Is—is she a great friend of yours?'

'No, but from your behaviour I can only assume that you wish her to be just that.'

She fetched the kettle and made the tea. 'I don't know what you mean . . .'

He took the kettle from her and put it back on the stove. 'Now, now, Debby, I'm sure that you have always impressed upon your little charges the necessity for speaking the truth; you should practice what you preach.'

She turned on him. 'How very unfair, and here have I been leaning over backwards, being understanding and tolerant—and not m-minding . . .'

She stopped just in time, indeed, she had said too much and she could have bitten off her tongue with chagrin. She said airily, not looking at him: 'I think

Barbara is very lovely and very witty—she made you laugh a great deal—well she made us all laugh—she's great fun.'

She glanced at him and although he looked poker faced, she was sure that he was amused about something. 'Well, we must have her as a frequent guest, mustn't we, Deborah, since you would like that?'

'I never said . . .' she began and interrupted herself to see to the muffins. It seemed prudent not to add to that; she busied herself with them, and then leading the way went to the drawing room where Eleanor was stretched on the rug before the fire, with the dogs leaning against her.

She jumped up as they went in. 'Miss Timmis said she'd love to have her tea upstairs but that she'd come down to collect it.'

'Run and fetch a tray love, and we'll get it ready for her and I'll take it up.' Deborah started to cut cake. 'I'll make a little pot of tea for her.'

Miss Timmis was almost embarrassingly grateful. 'Really, Mrs Beaufort, you shouldn't—I could have got tea for myself. I must say it's very pleasant sitting here with a book.'

'Visitors are fine, but tiring,' observed Deborah. 'We're going to loll round the fire and Eleanor's to stay up for dinner, so don't bother with anything until you hear the gong.'

Tea round the fire was a cheerful meal and if Deborah was a little quiet it passed unnoticed in Eleanor's happy chatter, and afterwards they played Scrabble until Deborah heard the Buckles' elderly Morris 1000 chug round the house and excused herself with the plea that she must go to the kitchen and make sure that everything was as it should be for the evening. She bore Eleanor upstairs presently to tidy herself for dinner and went to her own room to do her hair once more and add a little more make-up. She felt sick at the very idea of Barbara becoming a frequent visitor, that had been her own silly fault, too; she hadn't started off with such high ideals . . .

She called to Eleanor and went downstairs, to sit opposite Gideon, sipping her sherry, carrying on an empty conversation until Miss Timmis joined them, and the talk, centering round her forthcoming visit to her sister, became easier.

It surprised Deborah very much when Gideon stayed at home for the next two days, he worked in his study, writing a great deal and spending a lot of time telephoning so that they saw very little of him. All the same, it was nice to have him in the house, and at the end of the second day, he drove Miss Timmis to Salisbury to catch her train and when he got home, came straight to the drawing room where he showed Eleanor the rudiments of chess until Deborah carried her off for supper and bed. He was still there when she got back and laid himself out to be a charming companion for the rest of that evening. Deborah, in another new dress, aware that she looked her best, felt her hopes rising; he hadn't mentioned having weekend visitors, perhaps he found her a satisfying companion after all.

She might have known that it was nothing of the sort; they had watched the nine o'clock news together over their coffee and she had put aside her cup and picked up her sewing. Gideon asked her idly what she was making.

'Clothes for a doll I've got for Eleanor's Christmas present.'

'Ah—yes Christmas. We had better decide what we

intend to do—rather short notice to invite friends, but I've no doubt they'll accept. I expect you want to see something of your family. Decide what you want to do, will you and let me know? I'm going up to town tomorrow and I have a dinner date I don't care to break, but I'll give you a ring early the following morning. I must get seats for a Pantomime too, Eleanor's old enough to go to an evening performance so we'll make an occasion of it. That will give you a chance to wear a new dress . . .'

Deborah put down her sewing. There had been mockery in his voice and she couldn't bear that, it was as though he found it amusing that she should be trying to shake off her former staid image. She said quietly: 'I think it would make no difference what I wore. Not to you, at any rate; you think of me in nanny's uniform, don't you, Gideon? But I expected that.' She added fiercely: 'What else was there to expect?'

He was sitting back in his chair, staring at her with a calm face. 'Are you happy, Deborah?' He waved a large hand. 'Here? Do you find it too quiet? Peggy was asking me a day or so ago if you would like to take Eleanor for a visit; the twins would love to see you again and Eleanor likes being with them.'

She said in a wooden voice: 'That sounds delightful. If you're going to be in London, she won't miss you so much.'

'And you, Debby? Would you miss me?'

She eyed him stonily. 'I really don't think that my feelings come into it, nor do you have the least interest in them.'

She got up quickly and whisked out of the room and flew up the stairs, as she reached her room she heard the drawing room door open and Gideon's voice calling her, but she shut her door firmly on the sound.

Things were going from bad to worse and what a very good thing that he was going to London in the morning; she would have a headache and not go down until he had left and perhaps by the time he phoned . . . Perhaps what? she thought in a panic, and in the mean time he would have spent the evening with Barbara Inge. She ran a hot bath and lay in it until the water was cool, her thoughts whizzing round and round inside her head until the headache she was going to pretend to have in the morning was really there.

Indeed, it was still there when she woke after a brief, heavy nap towards morning so that she was able to tell Eleanor when the child came to her room, that she wouldn't be down to breakfast and would she see her father off. 'And I've taken something for my headache, love, so tell Daddy not to come up; I shall be asleep.'

To be on the safe side, she kept her eyes shut until she heard the car going down the drive.

Peggy Burns telephoned during the morning. 'Come for lunch,' she suggested when Deborah told her that Gideon wouldn't be home until the next day. 'And why not leave Eleanor here for the night—I'll drive her over in the morning—that'll give you time to get your plans laid for Christmas. I don't suppose you are doing much this year—you've not had the time—have you? But I expect there will be the usual family gatherings and so on.'

It was nice to have something to do; Deborah drove over later in the morning with Eleanor beside her. It was a cold grey day and she wondered if it was going to snow as she took the car the short distance; the day suited her mood, although she was cheered by Peggy's greeting of: 'Deborah, don't you look marvellous? That heavenly suit, and your hair is different!'

They had a boisterous lunch, with the twins allowed to sit at the table and Dee sleeping peacefully as usual. 'It isn't just you, Deborah, who looks smashing, it's Eleanor as well—she's plump and such a lovely healthy colour and so very happy. How's Gideon?'

'He is fine,' said Deborah. 'He works too hard, but he enjoys that, doesn't he? We had people for the weekend—he's a marvellous host . . .'

'Who came?'

Deborah told her, keeping her voice casual.

'Oh, is she still around?' asked Peggy Burns. 'The ghastly Barbara—always getting her talons in someone else's husband.' She gave Deborah a lightning glance. 'She's pretty good to look at, isn't she?'

'Fabulous, and such gorgeous clothes . . .'

'Well, as to that, you're not doing too badly yourself. Gideon must be so proud of you.'

Deborah couldn't think of an answer to this and Peggy went on kindly: 'Gideon's not always as busy as this; he tends to work in fits and starts; he's got a T.V. interview coming up—he's told you, of course, and that means making notes, but you'll be going to Brussels with him in the New Year, won't you? When is Miss Timmis coming back?'

Happily a question Deborah could answer: 'After Christmas; Gideon wants to send Eleanor to school—a day pupil of course—and I think she might like it, we're going to discuss it when he comes home.'

She left shortly after lunch. 'The Buckles have the afternoon off and the dogs will need a run before tea. Will you come to lunch tomorrow?'

'Tea, if I may. Can we all come?'

'Well of course; I'll get Mrs Buckle to make a chocolate cake. Please give my love to Mrs Beaufort when you see her.' Deborah began a round of hugs and kisses, ending with Eleanor who wanted to know anxiously if she would be lonely.

'I shall miss you, love, but I promise I won't be lonely—I've letters to write and I want to phone Granny Farley.'

The afternoon was melting rapidly into twilight by the time she got back to be welcomed rapturously by the dogs, their barks sounding hollowly in the empty house. She went indoors, changed into stout shoes, and went out of the back door, locking it behind her; the Buckles might be back before she returned but they had a key. With the dogs circling round her, she took the path which skirted the wood beyond the grounds at the back of the house. It was slippery with frost but she knew it well. It circled round the trees as it climbed the hill and came down the other side to join the lane to the village; half an hour's walk at the most, she would be back home before it grew dark.

She went fast, trying to outrun her unhappy thoughts and she was beginning the downhill rutted path on the other side of the wood when she noticed the Jack Russell, Benjy, was missing. She stopped and whistled and Jack and Prince whined. She hushed them and whistled and called again and this time she heard a faint bark, coming from somewhere within the wood. She had never penetrated its sombre depths but she did know that somewhere in its heart, towards the bottom of the hill, there was a pond. She whistled again, listened for Benjy's bark and then walked back a little way to where a narrow path led down into the trees. Jack and Prince came with her, walking sedately now, keeping to her heels as she began to slip and slide, barely able to see her way.

It seemed a very long way down and she stopped from time to time and called, to be answered by a whimper which sent her hurrying on once more.

The path ended at last, abruptly terminated by a pool of sluggish water, thinly coated with ice. Ice through which the unfortunate Benjy had fallen; she could see his small head turning desperately this way and that as he paddled in the broken ice, unable to get out because of the sheer sides of the pool. Jack and Prince barked and then went to the edge and whined, Deborah said: 'No, you don't. Stay, both of you.'

It was barely light by now, she cast around for some means of help and thankfully laid hands on a broken off branch, it was stout enough and there were any number of smaller branches on it, leafless now, but that was all to the good. She knelt down on the muddy ground and pushed the branch cautiously on to the water as near to Benjy's head as she could reach. He was a bright little dog and she prayed and hoped that he would have the sense to allow her to drag him to the edge . . .

'Get on the branches, love,' she begged him gently, 'just hang on and I'll pull you inside.'

For a few moments she thought that she must fail, but suddenly she felt his weight on the twigs as she scooped him up and then began to drag the branch back towards her. He fell off at once, and they had to start all over again but at last she had him at the pond's edge, but still out of reach. She shuffled backwards, hampered by Jack and Prince trying to help, and lifted the branch slowly, terrified that Benjy might drop off into the water again. But he didn't; with a yelp of delight he fell into her lap and shook himself, completing the ruin of her new suit. Not that she cared; she hugged him with relief while his friends nosed happily at them both. She didn't dare stay longer; she had moved round the pond and now she wasn't sure which path to take, there were several, barely discernible now, and anxious to get away from the pool she started up the first one she blundered into. It led uphill but twisted away after a few yards and presently, to her horror, it came to an abrupt end, barred by a towering thicket. She had Benjy in her arms, small and shivering and wet, and the other dogs crowded close to her. There was no help for it; they would have to go back—but not to the pond. She had seen a narrow track a short distance back, they would take that and hope for the best.

She found the track, but by now it was so dark that she could see nothing at all. Fighting panic, she stood still, deciding what was the best thing to do—the answer seemed to be to stay where she was. It was bitter cold and would get much colder as the night advanced, but surely if she and the dogs kept close together they would have a modicum of warmth. She felt around her and found a tree stump, icily cold but better than the damp, frosty ground. She perched on it, tucked Benjy under one arm and dragged Prince and Jack close on either side. They whined anxiously, but as they leaned against her their warmth was comforting.

Gideon had had a busy morning, indeed it was early afternoon before he stopped for sandwiches and beer eaten at his desk while he added a few more notes to the lecture he was to give later on in the week. These finished he sat back, not thinking of lectures at all, but of Deborah. He had expected to see her at breakfast that morning and when she hadn't come down he had felt a keen sense of disappointment, followed by an increasing desire to shake her until her teeth rattled for filling her head with such silly ideas, and an even greater desire to discover if she meant what she said. The more he considered this the more urgent it became to find out. He pushed his papers aside, asked his secretary to ring his home and when there was no answer, told her to try his sister's house, remembering that Eleanor and Deborah had been invited there.

Peggy answered the phone. 'Deborah? She left a couple of hours ago, Gideon, said she was going to take the dogs out and of course there's no one at home, she told me that she had given the Buckles the afternoon off since you weren't coming home and she would be on her own. Eleanor's here . . . She wants to talk to you.'

No one listening would have found the professor's manner anything but his usual urbane self. He talked to his small daughter for several minutes and then rang off.

'Cancel everything there is for the rest of the day, and that goes for my dinner date. I'm going home at once.'

His secretary had been with him for a long time. 'But sir—the rest of the afternoon appointments are easily postponed, but not this evening's—it's the Ministry . . .'

'I know, I know. Ring through and see if I can have a half an hour of someone's time now—explain—oh, say anything you can think of . . .'

She earned every penny of her excellent salary; within minutes he was in the Bentley driving down Whitehall.

The half hour stretched over an hour, only his

promise that he would return the following day made it possible for him to get away even then.

The evening rush hour was already under way as he crawled out of the city, showing no signs of impatience at the hold ups, but once on the M3 he kept up a steady seventy until he reached Salisbury and changed to the A30. In less than half an hour he was turning in through his own gates, to see lights shining from the house. Deborah was home.

She wasn't. The Buckles, delighted to see him, assured him that Mrs Beaufort hadn't returned from Mrs Burns, and when he rang Peggy it was only to hear her repeat what she had already said. 'And where are the dogs?' He wanted to know from Buckle.

'Possibly with Mrs Beaufort, sir. Although it's a little late . . . and dark . . .'

The professor grunted, shrugged himself into his sheepskin jacket, pulled on rubber boots, took the torch Buckle handed him, and left the house.

'Do you wish me to inform the police, sir?' asked Buckle at the door.

'I'll look round first; if the dogs are with Mrs Beaufort, she shouldn't be too hard to find.'

He tried the lane to the village first, with no success; then the grounds round the house, whistling for the dogs; half an hour had gone by by the time he started up the path by the wood, and it had begun to rain, a freezing downpour which made the going doubly difficult. He was at the top of the hill, circumventing the wood when he heard the dogs bark, and when he whistled, bark again.

Deborah was numb with cold and very frightened, even with the dogs for company the wood was giving her the creeps with its vague small rustlings and the steady drip of the rain. She had cried a little but since crying wasn't going to help, she had made herself stop and now sat huddled against the dogs' warm hairiness, sniffing and gulping and talking to them from time to time. When they barked she had let out a small yelp at the unexpectedness of it and it wasn't until they barked again, joyfully this time, that she heard the whistle. Gideon, come home by some miracle. She allowed herself the luxury of a few tears and forgot to wipe them away as the whistling grew louder and before very long gave way to the steady tramp of Gideon's feet. She could see the torch now and called out, but what with cold and fright her voice came out a useless squeak, lost among the rustling and dripping round her.

The torch's powerful light came to rest on her face, making her blink.

'You little fool,' said Gideon in such a rough voice that she winced. And then: 'Which one of you fell into the pool?'

She found a voice of sorts. 'Benjy.'

'You're soaked . . .'

'Well, I had to get him out.' She started to get to her feet and discovered to her embarrassment that her numbed legs wouldn't obey her. Gideon bent down and hauled her to her feet and bidding the dogs stay still, he began to rub her legs with hard hands. The pain of returning feeling brought the tears to her eyes again, and a small sob secretly escaped her. But it was only one; his, 'For God's sake, don't start snivelling,' was enough to choke back any desire to weep; if she could have laid hands on something suitable and heavy she might have been tempted to bang him over the head. To have spent the night in the miserable cold wetness of the wood could have been no worse than Gideon's even colder anger. His, 'Come along now,' was uttered so harshly that she gibbered with rage, but silently; if she said all the things on the tip of her tongue then he might turn round and walk away and leave her there. At the back of her head she knew quite well that he would never do such a thing, but it suited her at that moment to think so. She allowed herself to be led up an overgrown track, almost hidden by rough undergrowth, with Benjy tucked firmly under one arm and the glad dogs, their noses at Gideon's heels, crowding her on either side. Gideon didn't speak but went steadily ahead, holding fast to her hand and once or twice she felt sure that he must have lost the way, for the track seemed to go on for ever. And when they at last emerged at the top of the hill there wasn't much difference; the icy rain was still falling and the dark was stygian.

'Can you walk?' asked Gideon.

'Of course.' She strove to make her voice haughty and spoilt it with a sniff.

He hadn't let go of her hand but now he walked beside her, shining the torch ahead of them, highlighting the icy slipperyness of the path. She could see the lights from the house now and since there was no one to see allowed herself to weep from sheer thankfulness. By the time they reached the house she would be so wet that the tears would be unnoticed. She still had to explain exactly what had happened to Gideon even if he was in a rage. The bad temper could be accounted for, of course, Barbara had stood him up and he'd come home instead of spending the evening—or more than the evening?—with her. Well he could spend it alone as far as she was concerned. Deborah sniffed again; she had every intention of having a hot bath and going to bed.

The Buckles' reception made up to a large extent for

Gideon's terse greeting and lack of sympathy. Mrs Buckle bore her upstairs, tut-tutting all the way. A hot bath, hot soup, a glass of brandy and then a good hot dinner would soon put madam right, what a shame that the suit was a ruin, covered in mud and slime and smelling very nasty too. Deborah, soothed by the housekeeper's soft, country bred voice, turned to look down into the hall. Gideon, who had flung his jacket down, was examining Benjy, walking at the same time to the kitchen with Prince, Jack and Buckle behind him. He hadn't spoken to her, not even to ask if she was all right. He had behaved abominably; the hero in a romantic novel would have wrapped her in his sheepskin jacket and carried her all the way home, breathing easily too. Gideon had been breathing like a man under great stress and she had to admit, being a sensible girl, that if he had wrapped his jacket around her she would have dropped to the ground with the sheer weight of it. Besides, despite his size and strength, she and the jacket would have gravely impeded his way through the wood. She giggled and then burst into tears, something which Mrs Buckle saw with satisfaction. 'You'll feel better after a nice little cry, madam. You just sit down while I get these shoes off, and that suit.'

Deborah found herself in a hot bath, drinking brandy from the glass Mrs Buckle was proffering. 'I didn't have any tea, I shall be tight . . .'

Mrs Buckle urged her to drink it all. 'You get yourself dried, madam dear, and I'll fetch up a tray of tea at once. You can have it before you go down stairs. Dinner is put back half an hour so that the professor can change his clothes and see to the dogs.'

The brandy had set up a pleasant glow and, moreover, given her a lovely don't-care feeling.

Deborah did as she was told, and buttoned cosily into a russet velvet housecoat, emptied the teapot, and then, urged on by Mrs Buckle, went down stairs to the drawing room.

Gideon was standing in front of the fire with the dogs lying on the rug. He looked at her without speaking when she went in and she stopped just inside the door.

'I wouldn't have come down like this, but Mrs Buckle said you expected me . . . I—I won't stay.'

He smiled thinly. 'Afraid of me, Deborah?'

'Certainly not. I'd have stayed upstairs if I was. I expect you want to read me a lecture, so do get it off your chest, I don't expect it'll make much impression on me because I've drunk rather a lot of brandy and I feel a little light headed.' She was finding it much easier than she had expected thanks to the brandy and she added airily: 'I'm sorry your evening has been spoilt but I expect you can arrange another one; although she must be very much in demand.'

A kind of spasm swept over the professor's handsome features. 'Oh undoubtedly,' he agreed quietly.

'Well, it must be a bore for you having to come home instead of having an evening out,' went on Deborah kindly, egged on by the brandy, 'but I'm glad you did because I don't know what would have happened to the dogs.'

She came a little further into the room and sat down. 'I'm ready.'

Gideon bit back a laugh. 'I have no intention of blaming you, Deborah. I'm sorry I wasn't more sympathetic when I found you—I was—er—worried.'

'I expect you were; a whole evening spoilt.'

He let that pass. 'You were very brave to stay there

with the dogs—did it not enter your head to try and find a way out of the wood alone?'

'Alone? Without the dogs? Don't be silly, Gideon.'

He went over to the sofa table and filled a glass and gave it to her.

'You're right—I am silly—so silly that I haven't seen something right under my nose these past weeks.'

She said hastily: 'Oh, you're not all that silly really—I shouldn't have said that. I think you must be a very clever man—Peggy said so, besides you have so many friends.' She added for good measure, 'And they like you.'

'Do you like me, Deborah?'

She took a sip from her glass. 'Well, you know I do.' She was pleased to hear how coolly friendly her voice sounded. 'I wouldn't have married you if I hadn't liked you.'

'But the first time I asked you, you refused me out of hand. What made you change your mind I wonder?'

Her eyes flew to his face. 'You said you wouldn't ask me that.'

'Ah yes, I was forgetting. I phoned Eleanor while you were upstairs; she sent her love—she misses you.'

'She misses you too when you are not at home.'

He turned away to put his glass on the table. 'But that's why I married you, wasn't it, Deborah?' She didn't answer and he said briskly: 'Well, shall we have dinner?'

She had no appetite but she did her best, and made conversation when Buckle was in the room, lapsing into silence the moment he was out of it. Over coffee she asked: 'Are you staying tonight, Gideon?'

'But of course. I'll have to be in town tomorrow afternoon, but I'll go over to Peggy's and fetch Eleanor back for lunch, Peggy can come some other day.'

She nodded, thinking how delightful it was, sitting opposite him by the fire. She put down her coffee cup and sat back comfortably, feeling drowsy. A little too full of brandy and sherry and the glass of wine she had had with her dinner, she allowed her careful pretence to slip and smiled at Gideon, her face made beautiful by love. The next moment she was almost asleep. Gideon sat watching her; Buckle came in, removed the tray soundlessly and crept out again; an hour later he returned, it was, after all, almost eleven o'clock and time to lock up for the night.

'Come back in ten minutes, Buckle,' the professor said quietly, 'I'll carry Mrs Beaufort upstairs—she's tired out.'

'Mrs Buckle wanted to know if madam would want anything for the night?' whispered Buckle, 'she's in the kitchen . . .'

'Very kind of her, but I fancy sleep is the only thing my wife needs.'

He sat a little longer after Buckle had gone and then got up, scooped Deborah up gently and carried her upstairs and into her room. He stood for a minute looking down at her, her sandy hair spread over her shoulder, still deeply asleep, indeed snoring in a faint ladylike manner.

She didn't stir as he laid her on the bed and pulled the quilt over her, arranging her hair neatly on the pillow and then stooping to kiss her gently. She looked enchanting and he paused to admire her curling eyelashes before he went quietly to the door, turning out all the lights except the small lamps on either side of the bed. He went back again and poured water into a glass and left it within reach; she would probably wake with a blinding headache.

CHAPTER NINE

DEBORAH woke in the very early hours of the morning with a mild headache and a raging thirst. Still half asleep, she sat up in bed, drank the water Gideon had so thoughtfully left for her, wondered for about fifty seconds why she was still in her housecoat and then turned over and went to sleep again. When she woke again it was to find Molly, the daily housemaid, drawing back the curtains, and her tea tray on the bedside table. Her headache had gone and as she drank her tea she recalled the previous evening. Someone had carried her up to bed and since neither Mrs Buckle nor Buckle were physically capable of that, it must have been Gideon. She sighed; no wonder he stayed in London if she had so little to offer in the way of companionship. Just how unglamorous can I get? she asked herself crossly, snoring my head off in a dressing gown. The thought sent her out of bed, to shower and dress in a dashing pleated skirt with a matching waistcoat over a silk shirt which had cost the earth and was worth every penny. And because she wanted to get down to breakfast quickly she tied her hair back with a ribbon and hurried downstairs.

Gideon was standing with his back to the fire, the dogs at his feet. His good-morning was affable and when she thanked him rather diffidently for seeing her safely into her bed, he shrugged. 'Think nothing of it,' he told her lightly. Over breakfast he asked her if she had any plans for the next few days.

'Why no—well, shopping for Christmas, but nothing arranged.'

'Good. I'm taking a few days off. I'll be back tonight—but late—don't wait up. If you like we could drive over and see Mother tomorrow and leave Eleanor for a couple of days. She likes to stay with her Granny and do her shopping.'

'Yes, of course. Does she know?'

'I'll tell her this morning—have you any messages for Peggy?'

'Only my love and thanks for having Eleanor.'

He was back with Eleanor before lunch, a meal he didn't stay for. 'No time,' he observed, 'I must be at the office by half-past two and it's already well past eleven o'clock.' He kissed Eleanor and then crossed the room to touch Deborah's cheek briefly. 'We'll leave after breakfast in the morning—will you pack a few things for Eleanor? Oh, and if you take the dogs for a walk this evening, take a torch and keep to the lanes.'

She heard him come home very late that evening, entering the house very quietly, pausing in the hall where Buckle had put a tray with a thermos jug of coffee on the side table, and then going to his study. She stayed awake until she heard him come upstairs twenty minutes later; only then did she curl up and go to sleep.

The dogs went with them in the morning, crowding into the back of the Bentley with Eleanor while Deborah sat beside Gideon. The little girl did most of the talking; planning her shopping, excited that she was to visit Mrs Beaufort, describing the shops in Milsom Street and what she intended to buy. She and Deborah were still deep in a friendly argument as to the best colour to choose for a scarf for Mrs Buckle when they reached Mrs Beaufort's house.

They received a warm welcome. 'Never felt better in my life!' declared Mrs Beaufort in answer to Deborah's enquiries. 'Let's have coffee first then you shall go to your room, Eleanor—the same one as usual. I daresay Deborah will help you to unpack.'

Presently, when the unpacking was done, they went downstairs again. Deborah saw that mother and son were deep in conversation, so she suggested at once that she and Eleanor should take the dogs into the garden. It was a cold morning but brightened by thin sunshine, she put on her brown top coat, tied a scarf round her head, buttoned Eleanor into her coat, and went outdoors, where they threw twigs for the dogs and ran races over the grass.

Gideon, sitting facing the windows, watched the distant figures and presently his mother stopped in mid-sentence and smiled because he didn't notice her silence. 'It is delightful to see little Eleanor so happy,' she remarked in a mild voice. 'Such a change in the child—she loves her stepmother, doesn't she?' She picked up her embroidery from the table beside her chair. There were other questions she would have liked to have asked, but a quick glance at her son's expressionless face stopped her. 'What are your plans for Christmas?' she asked cheerfully, 'I hear that you had friends for the weekend—perhaps you plan a houseparty?'

He shook his head, not looking away from the window. 'No—I don't know, Mother . . .'

And that, thought Mrs Beaufort, was so unlike Gideon's well ordered life, something, or someone, must have thrown him off balance. She followed his gaze out of the window, to where Deborah and Eleanor were standing arm in arm, laughing their heads off about something or other, and smiled gently.

They left the little girl with her grandmother after lunch, and started on the drive back to Tollard Royal. The short day was losing its brightness already and there was a nip in the air. Deborah, snug in her coat, settled back beside Gideon. It had been a pleasant lunch and they had all laughed a lot and Gideon had teased Eleanor gently and she had giggled and cheeked him back; it was hard to think of her as the rather solemn little girl she had first known, and her grandmother had noticed it too, for she had said as she kissed Deborah good-bye: 'What miracles you have done for that child, Deborah—she's really happy. I do hope you're just as happy, dear.'

Deborah thought about that as they drove along. It seemed impossible to be happy and unhappy at the same time, but she was; happy to be with Gideon, however briefly, happy to be his wife, even if she wasn't, happy to have Eleanor and a lovely home. And unhappy because she meant so little to him. Oh, he liked her all right, he had even once or twice since she had started to dress well, looked at her with a look of surprise on his face, as though he'd never really seen her before. Not that she could ever hope to compete with Lady Barbara's beauty. But that didn't mean that she wouldn't try; she had enough money, that thanks to Gideon's generosity. She heaved a small sigh and he said gently: 'What's the matter, Deborah?'

'Nothing,' she spoke too quickly.

'Would you like to stop for tea, or wait until we're home?'

'Oh, home, I think—besides Mrs Buckle made you a fruit cake when I told her you'd be home for a day or two.' She hesitated, 'But perhaps you've plans . . .'

He said very evenly: 'Why do you imagine that I

find your company so boring that I should wish to leave the house the moment I get back into it?'

'I don't—I mean . . . That is, you've lots of friends, people you've known for years—shared interests, and—and that sort of thing.'

'And so, do we have no shared interests?' His voice was placid but he was driving too fast.

'Eleanor,' said Deborah promptly and thought what an awkward conversation they were having. 'And you love your home and so do I—and the dogs and . . .'

'Yes?' he prompted.

'I can't think of anything else at the moment.'

'A mutual liking?' He asked blandly.

'Well, naturally.'

'Nothing more?' She mistrusted the silkiness of his voice. She gazed out of the window and wondered what he would say if she told him that she loved him. 'Nothing more,' she told him steadily.

After that they didn't exchange more than a few words, and those quite impersonal. They talked like two strangers over their tea and then the phone rang and he went away to answer it, not coming back. Deborah, anxious to occupy her mind, sat down at the desk in the drawing room and addressed Christmas cards, rang her mother and then went upstairs to tidy herself for the evening. She got back to the drawing room to find Gideon already there with Buckle. They were in their shirt sleeves, erecting a large Christmas tree in the wide bay window at the end of the room and just for the moment she forgot that they weren't on the best of terms and hurried over to admire it. 'Oh, how super—shall we decorate it this evening?'

'Eleanor and I have done it together ever since she was a toddler.'

He spoke pleasantly but she felt her cheeks redden

at the snub. All the same she said quickly: 'Oh, of course—it'll be ready for her to help you when she gets home. It's a magnificent tree.'

'We have left our plans for Christmas rather late this year, but the tree is something we can't overlook.'

Buckle murmured something and Gideon replied with a cheerful: 'Well, since I'm at home for a couple of days, I daresay we can get organized. We'll have to have some friends in for drinks.' He glanced across to where Deborah was standing uncertainly, watching them. 'There are half a dozen invitations in today's post—they are on my desk if you would like to look through them?'

He stood back, surveying his handiwork with Buckle beside him. 'We're just about finished here— I'll be back to pour our drinks in ten minutes or so.'

She went along to the study, feeling like a child who'd been dismissed back to the schoolroom. And yet Gideon hadn't actually said anything unkind; merely put her where she supposed she belonged—in the outer perimeter of his life. She went over to his desk and picked up the little pile of cards and looked at the first one, not seeing a word because her eyes were full of tears. She hadn't thought it would be like this, being held at arm's length, reminded, oh, so politely, that he had married her for Eleanor's sake and for no other reason. She even doubted now if he liked her; hadn't he called her a fool that evening when she had got lost in the wood—his voice had been rough, and he'd been angry although later he had been kind enough.

She was shaken out of her dreary, depressing thoughts by the opening of the door, and before she had time to wipe away her tears, Gideon was beside her.

He had seen them, of course, although she had turned away her head. He took the cards from her and laid them on the desk. 'Now why should a handful of invitations make you cry?' he wanted to know.

Because she wasn't looking at him she didn't see the gleam in his eyes and since his voice was calmly deliberate and nothing more she was filled with icy despair. 'Nothing,' she mumbled, and then, like a child, 'I should like to go to Dorchester ...'

She didn't see his bitter little smile, either. 'Running home to mother, dear?'

He had never called her that. She wished with all her heart that she was his dear. 'No, Gideon—only if you wanted me to go ...'

The gleam in his eyes turned into a blaze. 'How long have we been married?' he wanted to know, 'A couple of weeks—not much more ...'

She didn't answer although she could have told him down to the last minute.

'And you think that I am regretting our marriage already?'

Deborah had mastered the tears except for an odd sniff or so. 'Perhaps. You see, in theory it was a splendid idea, and I know that Eleanor is happy now, and that's what you wanted, didn't you? But in practice I don't fit in, do I? Your friends ... They're clever and witty and I don't know them.' She sighed. 'I can't compete.'

'With what or whom?' He interrupted.

'Everything,' she said simply. 'This!' She swept an arm around the handsome, solidly furnished room. 'Money, comfort, your lovely house, driving around in a Bentley,' and because she was an honest girl 'and Lady Barbara Inge ...'

The professor said 'Ha!' in a fierce voice, 'and now

we come to the root of the matter. Could it possibly be that you are jealous, Debby?'

She made an instant denial, not looking at him. 'That's ridiculous, how could I be jealous when I don't—that is—there has to be a reason . . .'

'You're very mealy mouthed all of a sudden. What you haven't the nerve to say is that one has to love someone to be jealous of them.' His voice was silky. 'I'm sure you must agree with me.'

'Yes—no, I don't know.' She could feel the tears crowding into her throat again. She whispered: 'Please could we not talk about it any more?' And fate for once gave her a helping hand in the shape of Buckle, coming to warn them that dinner had been ready to serve for the last ten minutes, adding reproachfully: 'I sounded the gong madam.'

'Oh, Buckle, we're so sorry—we just didn't hear it.' She slipped past him and into the dining room with Gideon silent beside her and nibbled at Mrs Buckle's excellent dinner without really eating anything, carrying on a half witted conversation at the same time. She was only vaguely aware of what she was talking about, but anything was better than silence. True, after a while Gideon responded, egging her on gently, the corners of his rather grim mouth twitching. She was quite worn out by the time they left the table, her head empty of words, for the life of her she was unable to stop the relieved sigh when he told her that he had some work to do and would go to the study. He heard it and stopped on his way from the room saying curtly: 'I shall be working late—we shall see each other at breakfast. Goodnight, Deborah.'

She mumbled her own goodnight and sat down by the fire, looking composed. She even smiled, but too late, he'd already closed the door behind him.

Then she sat there, doing nothing, although there were still a few presents to wrap, and even last minute Christmas cards to do. She had forgotten them entirely while she tried to decide what to do. Obviously the matter couldn't rest; she and Gideon would have to have a talk. Something could be worked out and in a sensible fashion; she didn't think that he wanted to be rid of her, he had wanted a mother for Eleanor and she knew without conceit that she had more than come up to his expectations. On the other hand, if she hadn't fallen in love with him, she would have taken Barbara as a matter of course and not minded over much, although he should have told her that he was in love with her, she frowned, but when they had married, he hadn't known about Barbara's return from America, had he?

She went upstairs to her room and got ready for bed. She had made a fine mess of everything, now how to put it right? No amount of thinking helped; she slept at length, her head a kaleidoscope of highly colourful fancies.

Morning brought common sense and pride to the rescue, as well as a nagging fear at the back of her mind that Gideon might have wondered why she had suddenly become such a weepy, waspish young woman, quite unlike her most normal calm, quiet self. Something which must be nipped in the bud at once.

He was coming into the hall from the kitchen, the dogs at his heels, as she got downstairs and she didn't waste a moment in putting her resolution into effect. Her good-morning was cheerful, friendly and brisk; she followed it up with a remark about the weather, a grey stormy morning which didn't merit mention, anyway, and then sat herself down to breakfast.

Gideon had wished her good-morning, accepted his

cup of coffee and begun on his post. She began on her own breakfast in silence, thinking sadly that she might just as well not have been there and then telling herself bracingly that self pity wasn't going to do her a ha'p'orth of good, so she opened her own letters and read them through several times until he put the last of his mail down and passed her several cards.

'More invitations—we had better accept these, I think, and give a party after Christmas.'

'So I'll accept them all?'

'Yes, if you will. And we still have to decide about Christmas. Eleanor has always stayed either with Peggy or my mother and I've joined her for a few days, but we shall have to change that, shan't we?'

Here was an opportunity for her to let him see that she was still the sensible, undemanding girl that he had married. 'I expect you took the opportunity to visit your friends—well, I'll be here with Eleanor—I mean, she need not stay with Mrs Beaufort or Peggy and I expect you'll be here for some of the time . . .' Her voice trailed away under his ferocious stare.

'You talk arrant nonsense Deborah.' He gathered up his letters and got up and stalked out of the room, leaving her to stare at her plate. She discovered that she wasn't only angry, but that she was very unhappy too. After a few minutes' thought she got up quickly and marched across the hall and flung the study door open without knocking.

Gideon was standing at the french window, staring out into the garden. He looked over his shoulder with a frown and then raised his brows in surprise, but before he could speak, Deborah said very flatly: 'I'm going to see Mother, I'll take the presents and stay for lunch.'

She flew out again and galloped up the stairs, fearful

YEAR'S HAPPY ENDING   187

that he might come after her, but he didn't and she felt
quite irrational disappointment.

She put on her splendid coat, found scarf, handbag
and gloves then went almost stealthily downstairs,
anxious not to meet Gideon. But before she went she
would have to see Mrs Buckle and arrange for his
lunch; she went to the kitchen and Mrs Buckle, asked
to produce lunch for her master, nodded uncertainly.
'So he won't be going with you madam?'

'Well, no, Mrs Buckle—he has some work he wants
to finish.'

'I see madam—and Christmas? What will the
arrangements be? There's not much time?'

Deborah said hastily: 'Yes, I know—I'm sorry Mrs
Buckle, but we'll let you know this evening—I'll be
back this afternoon and we'll talk about it then.'

'Right, madam,' said Mrs Buckle and glanced out of
the window. 'Nasty weather blowing up if you ask me,
will you be driving the Mini?'

'Yes it's quite a short trip and I know the road very
well.'

She smiled and went through the door into the back
lobby of the house where everyone kept their macs and
wellies and dog leads hung on the wall; out of sight
were the keys for the Mini and the Buckles' car.

Deborah stretched out a hand. There was only one
set of keys and they weren't for the Mini. They were
not on the floor either, she got down on her knees to
make sure.

'They are in my pocket, Deborah,' said Gideon
behind her, and she scrambled to her feet, furious at
being found grovelling. She put out a hand word-
lessly, but he didn't give her the keys, instead he
caught her hand in his and held it fast. 'I'll drive
you, Debby. There's bad weather on the way, and

even if the sun were blazing from a blue sky, I would still drive you.'

'Why?' asked Deborah and seeing his face, caught her breath, closed her beautiful eyes and opened them again just to make sure. He was looking at her as though she were something precious to be cherished; there was no mockery in his face now only an intentness and a question. Suddenly all the things she had longed to say and had kept bottled up, came pouring out; she didn't care any more what he might think or say, if only he would go on looking like that for ever.

'I've made a fine hash of things,' the words tripped off her tongue and she made no attempt to stop them. 'I truly didn't mean to, you know and it would have been all right if I hadn't fallen in love with you, I mean I wouldn't have minded about you always being away and looking at me as though I wasn't there and Lady Barbara Inge . . .'

She choked to a stop because Gideon's great chest was heaving with laughter. 'Oh, you . . .' she cried and thumped him with her free hand, to have it caught and gently held. He had both her hands now, she tugged at them, but he pulled her close and put his arms around her, holding her very tightly.

'Hush,' he said in a voice as gentle as his hands had been. 'Listen to me, my dearest girl. I don't know when I first discovered that I loved you; I suppose it must have been from the first moment we met, only I didn't realise—you grew on me, slowly, until you were with me all the time, wherever I was. Most disconcerting it was, I can tell you. And the more I loved you the more difficult I found it to say so; I tried teasing you to be met with your most nannyish airs, I tried telling myself that I would get over what was no more than an infatuation, only my God it wasn't—it isn't. I've never loved anyone in my life as I love you, darling, my darling. There isn't a woman who can hold a candle to you.'

He bent and kissed her hard and then gently, and Deborah slid her arms round his neck and kissed him back. When she had her breath she started: 'Lady Ba . . .'

'Oh, lord, not her again,' declared Gideon, 'unwitting bait, sweetheart, to try and trap you into letting me see your real feelings.'

'You never guessed?'

He shook his head. 'No, but just once or twice I hoped . . .' He kissed her again and Mrs Buckle opened the door, gave a surprised squawk and began to retreat. Gideon didn't loosen his hold on Deborah. 'Ah, Mrs Buckle—we shall both be out for lunch, and while we are gone, you may start making plans for Christmas and don't tell me that there isn't enough time. Spend what you want to. My wife and I will arrange the details while we are at her mother's and let you know this evening.'

Mrs Buckle nodded speechlessly and disappeared as Deborah said: 'But Gideon, darling, how can we at the last minute . . .'

'Say that again my love.'

'At the last minute . . .'

'Quite easily. Say that again, darling.'

'At the last minute?'

'Not that bit . . .'

'Gideon, darling,' said Deborah and was kissed for her pains.